LADY EMMA'S REVENGE

Lady Emma Stanton is determined to discover who killed her husband, even if it means enlisting the assistance of a Bow Street Runner. Sergeant Samuel Ross is no gentleman; he has rough manners and little time for etiquette. So when Emma and Sam decide the best way to ferret out the criminal is to pose as husband and wife, they are quite the mismatched pair. Soon, each discovers they have growing feelings for the other — but an intimate relationship across such a social divide is out of the question . . .

FENELLA J. MILLER

LADY EMMA'S REVENGE

Complete and Unabridged

LINFORD
Leicester

First published in Great Britain in 2015

First Linford Edition
published 2016

A catalogue record for this book is available
from the British Library.

ISBN 978–1–4448–3091–0

Published by
F. A. Thorpe (Publishing)
Anstey, Leicestershire

Set by Words & Graphics Ltd.
Anstey, Leicestershire
Printed and bound in Great Britain by
T. J. International Ltd., Padstow, Cornwall

This book is printed on acid-free paper

For Rachel, Emma and Hannah.

1

Chelmsford, 1816

The crack of the pistol shot echoed through the house. Emma stumbled backwards, almost losing her balance and crashing headlong down the staircase.

The sound had come from Richard's study. Gathering up her skirts, she spun and raced down the stairs, across the vast expanse of chequered floor and along the spacious passageway that led to his sanctum.

His man of business, Stokes, barred her way as she tried to go in. 'No, my lady, better not see. I was too late to stop him.' He wiped his eyes on his sleeve but remained firmly in front of the closed door. 'The master is dead. There's nothing you can do for him.'

'Dead? Are you telling me that he has killed himself? I don't understand — we

1

breakfasted together little more than an hour ago and he was perfectly well.' Her head was spinning; she couldn't take in this dreadful news.

The housekeeper, Smithson, appeared beside her. 'You come along with me, my lady. Let Mr Stokes take care of things. He'll get Dr Reynolds to deal with this.'

Emma allowed herself to be gently guided away from the study. She had believed her husband had been contented with their union despite his lack of interest in the marriage bed. How could he have taken his own life? It made no sense.

'No, Smithson, I'll not be removed so easily. Mr Stanton could not possibly have committed suicide. I must speak to Stokes, and he must send for the magistrate and have him investigate the matter.'

Ignoring the anxious tutting and clucking from her housekeeper, she hurried back to the study and turned the handle — but the door was locked.

She banged on the door and demanded to be let in, and she was certain she heard movement behind the door.

Stokes rushed to her side, his face pale. 'I locked the door, my lady. The master wouldn't want you to see him like that.'

'There's someone in there. Quickly, unlock the door — whoever it is will be getting away.'

His expression changed to one of concern and he fumbled in his pocket for the missing key. 'There cannot be anyone inside, my lady. The door has been locked and the windows are closed.'

Eventually the door was opened, and Emma was first to enter. The room was indeed empty, but she was certain there had been somebody inside. Her attention turned to her husband, who was slumped across the desk, his fair hair caked with blood, the discharged duelling pistol in his hand.

Emma's eyes filled and she swayed. Then she dug her nails into her palms. She would not faint; she must be strong. Richard had been murdered, and she could think of only one person who would wish to do this. His younger half-brother, Benedict Stanton, had always coveted the estates and substantial income that went with them. The last time Richard had spoken to his brother had been more than a year ago, and the meeting had ended with Benedict threatening to kill him.

'I cannot go any closer. Stokes, could you check the desk and see if there is a note for me?'

After a cursory search amongst the papers, he shook his head. 'Nothing at all, my lady. The master would have left a note explaining. I don't understand.'

'I am feeling decidedly unwell and must lie down for a while. I shall leave you to speak to the doctor. Would you also send word to our lawyers? They must bring the will. Thank God the estates are not entailed. They will remain under my control and will not be passed on to Mr Stanton.'

'The master had summoned me here

on an urgent matter,' Stokes said. 'I did not get the opportunity to speak to him, but he received two letters from London this morning, and I believe it was in relation to those that he wished to speak to me.' He bowed and stepped aside to allow her to exit.

Smithson was waiting in the passage-way and Emma was glad of her support. The shock and anger at Richard's demise had carried her through the first awful minutes, but now grief was overwhelming her. It was as if she had been shrouded in a heavy, wet cloak. Her feet were becoming more difficult to move, and a welcome blackness took her away.

* * *

Bridge Street, London

Sam Ross had been up all night apprehending two villains wanted for the murder of a fellow runner. His eyes were gritty from lack of sleep, his hands blood-smeared and his clothes little better. He slumped into a chair, and Meg, the girl who took care of his rooms, placed a steaming bowl of porridge in front of him followed by a mug of porter.

'You get this down you, Sergeant. You look done in. Did you catch them varmints?'

'I did, but I must wash before I eat.' He was about to shove himself to his feet, but she pushed him back. 'You stop where you are, sir. I'll fetch you a basin and some hot water.' The porridge and beer were whisked away and immediately replaced with what he needed.

The water was red-stained by the time Sam had finished his ablutions. He dried himself and handed the damp towel to Meg. He was about to spoon up the last delicious mouthful of his meal when he heard footsteps on the stairs that led to his door.

'See who that is,' he told Meg. 'No doubt it will be bad news of some sort.' He wiped his mouth and drained the last of his porter. His maid hurried to

6

answer the loud knocking, and Sam was unsurprised to see the shrivelled form of the clerk from Bow Street sidle in.

'What do you want, Garfield? I've only just got back, dammit, and I've yet to find my bed.'

'I beg your pardon, Sergeant Ross, but Mr Fletcher requires your immediate attendance.'

'Tell him he'll have to wait. I'll be with him by noon. If the matter is too urgent to stand for a few hours, then let him give the task to somebody else. There are dozens of us working out of Bow Street nowadays. Let one of them take this case.'

The clerk was about to argue but wisely thought better of it. 'I shall give Mr Fletcher your message, but he will not be pleased by it.'

Sam waved him away and Garfield scuttled off like the beetle he was. Then he yawned, and without further ado headed for his bedchamber. His lodgings were in Bridge Street, no more than a ten-minute walk from where the magistrate held court. He was lucky he had sufficient funds from his days as a soldier to pay for decent lodgings, for he was damn sure he would not live as well on the meagre wages he earned as a runner. Since he'd returned from Waterloo last summer, he'd immediately applied to join them. He needed something physical to do; something to take his mind off the loss of his two closest friends in the bloody battle.

'Meg, wake me at half past eleven, and not a minute before.'

'You go along to your bed, Sergeant. I'll get your garments sponged and pressed whilst you sleep. It ain't right how they treat you; you never have a minute to yourself.'

'I am a lead investigator; the penalty of being efficient at one's job is to be asked for by name.'

Meg followed him into his bedchamber, and with her assistance he removed his boots and outer garments and flopped into bed. He was instantly asleep.

Emma awoke to find her maid, Annie, sitting at her side. 'I wish to get up. Has the doctor visited, do you know?'

'He has indeed, my lady. He left you a tisane to take that will help you sleep.'

'I have no wish to sleep any longer. Help me get dressed, then send for Stokes.'

Emma was pacing her sitting room when Richard's man of business arrived. 'Come in, and I apologise for my weakness earlier,' she said to him. 'I'm quite recovered and will not let my emotions overwhelm me again.' He seemed reluctant to step into her private room, but she beckoned him impatiently. 'We cannot stand on ceremony, Stokes. I wish to know what transpired with the doctor. Was he prepared to sign the death certificate as an accident?'

'He was happy to do so, my lady. The coffin was fetched from the vault, Mrs Smithson took care of things, and now the master is resting in the family chapel.' He cleared his throat and refused to meet her eye. 'Sir Reginald sent his man over and has decided to take the matter no further. Investigation will only serve to draw attention to the suicide.'

'Suicide? I told you my husband was murdered, and if Sir Reginald is not prepared to investigate, then I shall take matters into my own hands. I have no intention of inviting the remnants of Richard's family to attend the funeral, and I am estranged from my own. Therefore, I wish to hold it as soon as it can be arranged.'

'The vicar has called in, my lady, and the service can be held tomorrow. The master will be interred in the family vault, so there's no necessity to employ a gravedigger.'

Talk of such things almost brought her to her knees. She could only bear the thought of Richard's death if she pushed it to the back of her mind and concentrated her efforts on seeking re-venge. 'I shall have a letter for London as soon as I have penned it. I'm going to be in the study and will send for you there.'

His shocked expression almost made her retract her statement. For a recently bereaved widow to enter the room in which the death of her husband had taken place was unheard of. However, Richard had always given her free rein to do as she pleased, and she had no intention of changing her character just because he was no longer with her.

Somehow she had expected the house to reflect the death of its master, but the sun still shone through the windows, the tall vases of summer flowers still scented the entrance hall, and the staff appeared to be going about their daily business as usual.

The study door was closed, and it took all of Emma's courage to reach out and turn the handle. She doubted she would ever visit this room again once the murder was solved. Richard had received a missive from London, and she needed to find this before she wrote to the magistrate at Bow Street and requested that his most efficient investigator come to her immediately.

After a fruitless search, she realised the letter was no longer in the study. A shiver flickered down her spine. Had Richard been killed because of this? The family lawyers resided in Chelmsford, a sizeable market town no more than five miles distant, so this communication could not have come from them.

After writing her letter she sanded it, folded it neatly and pressed the Stanton ring into the molten wax to seal it. Her husband had never worn this, but kept it in a drawer and used it only on his correspondence. She pulled the bell-strap and when Stokes appeared she handed him the letter, plus a sovereign to cover the exorbitant expense of sending it by express.

He could not fail to notice to whom it was addressed, but he merely shrugged and set off to do her bidding. After he had departed to run her errand, she began a thorough exploration of Richard's papers. She was aware that his funds were invested in various manufactories and shipping lines, and the reports from these showed a healthy profit. Whitford Hall, and the various estates which belonged with it, were also showing a handsome return.

She carefully replaced all the account books, and various letters appertaining to these subjects, in the desk. A parlourmaid had already scrubbed the top clean, and if she had not known that less than four hours ago it had been covered with her husband's blood, Emma would have thought there was nothing amiss.

This room would remain untouched until the Bow Street Runner arrived and could examine it himself. The lawyers would have to meet her in the small drawing room; the study was out of bounds. She carefully locked the door and put the key in her pocket, as she had no wish for anyone, even Stokes, to be in the study until it had been properly examined.

The weather was perfect for an

afternoon walk around the rose garden. She had not the energy to change into her riding habit and take her massive gelding for a gallop. As she wandered amongst these sweet-smelling flowers, she ran through the practicalities of her situation. Richard had shown her his will; she held title to everything, with no trustees or legal impediment. It would be highly unusual for a female to hold the reins of such a large estate, but for some reason a widow was considered more capable than an unmarried lady.

She settled in a concealed arbour, breathing in the smell of honeysuckle and roses, and allowing the warmth of the sun to thaw her icy limbs. When she had rejected her father's choice of husband he had disowned her. The Earl of Streford would not be gainsaid, and he ordered her to be sent to live with an ancient relative in Scotland. So Emma had accepted Richard's offer. She had not been in love with him, but had liked him well enough.

Love had not grown over the five years, as they had spent little time together. Richard had preferred to be with his male friends and was often away from home with them. However, Emma's life was infinitely better than before her marriage, and she had been relatively happy.

Whoever had taken Richard from her would pay dearly. She would not rest until she had found the culprit and brought him to justice. She was convinced that the murderer was Benedict Stanton — all she had to do was prove it. When the vile creature had visited she had not met him, but she would never forget his voice, or the venom with which he had issued his threats. At the time, she had been concealed behind a pillar in the entrance hall — not intending to eavesdrop, but merely keeping out of the way of someone Richard had said was a nasty and objectionable character.

The death of her husband would not be announced in the *Times*; the burial would be private. They were a considerable distance from the village, and the staff were loyal and would not discuss the matter if asked to keep it private. With luck, Mr Stanton would not hear of it. She jerked upright at the stupidity of her thoughts. Of course he would hear of it — he was the perpetrator, wasn't he? This would make things so much easier to prove — if the villain appeared in the next few days insisting that he was now the legal owner of the Stanton estates, and a mere woman could not possibly inherit them her own right, she would know for sure he had done the deed.

The only person who might reveal that Richard was dead was the vicar himself. She scrambled to her feet and ran headlong to the house. She must ride at once to the vicarage and make sure he held his tongue. This should not prove problematical, as his living was provided by the Stanton estates, and he would not wish to offend the person who paid his stipend.

2

Sam shouldered his way past the press of miscreants who were being processed for the courtroom, greeted several of his fellow runners, and fought his way to the staircase at the rear of the building. Mr Fletcher, who was the magistrate in charge of Bow Street, had his office on the first floor away from the noise and unpleasantness downstairs.

The clerk was hovering in the anteroom, glancing nervously at the wall clock, which now showed it was fifteen minutes past the hour of twelve o'clock. Sam ignored him. The man was undoubtedly efficient, but he was sly, and no more honest than those in the cells beneath them.

Mr Fletcher was standing at the window staring down the street, but he turned at once and greeted him. 'At last. Forgive me for dragging you from your bed, Sergeant, but this is a matter of the most extreme urgency.' He gestured towards a chair. 'Sit down, man, sit down. I shall give you the letter that came by express this morning to read for yourself.'

The paper was expensive, the penmanship immaculate. The address at the top was Whitford Hall — not somewhere Sam was familiar with. He perused the missive and his eyes brightened. 'A man murdered in a locked room, and letters missing. This sounds like an intriguing case.' He continued until he'd read the whole. The remuneration offered was substantial; the lady who had written to ask for their help was the widow of the man who had been killed.

'I shall leave at once, sir, as this seems a matter of the utmost urgency. It is no more than half a day's ride to Chelmsford. I'll overnight there and make a few discreet enquiries about the family before I go on to meet Mrs Stanton.'

'Take someone else with you of your choice, but you have to pay him from your own pocket. Keep me informed of developments. There is no need to return until the matter is solved satisfactorily.'

'If Collins is available, I'll take him. We've worked together before and he's a shrewd fellow, able to blend in and worm out useful information from the locals.' Sam's chair scraped as he stood. 'Did Mrs Stanton request me by name?'

'No. She asked for my best investigator.' Fletcher waved him away and resumed his stare out of the window.

Sam moved silently to the door and threw it open. As he expected, Garfield had been lurking behind it, and was sent flying. Serve him right for eavesdropping; the Beak had been told several times that his clerk was dishonest, but he refused to send him packing. He had said that it was a good thing to have a foot in both camps, so to speak.

It took a while to locate Collins, who was in a local hostelry drowning his sorrows after failing to apprehend the collector he had been sent after. Highwaymen were difficult to catch at the best of times, and this one was proving particularly elusive. His bright red waistcoat immediately identified him as a mounted runner, and Sam was not surprised there was a noticeable gap on either side of Collins.

'Collins, I've a job out of town. You're to come with me. Lose the waistcoat, dress plainly and bring your barking irons. We have a murder to solve — I'll tell you more about it as we ride. Be ready to leave in an hour.'

'Right you are, Sergeant. I'll be glad to get out of this hellhole for a while. Have you squared it with the Beak?'

'Of course. I'll pay your expenses and give you a couple of sovereigns — if there are any left over when we're done.'

★ ★ ★

Fortunately the vicar had not had time to gossip about Richard's death, and Emma returned to Whitford Hall satisfied she had stemmed any possible tittle-tattle. The letter she had sent to London should arrive at its destination with an hour or two, and the investigator she had sent for should be with them by tomorrow morning at the latest.

Whoever it was would have to attend the funeral, which was to be held tomorrow afternoon. It was going to be difficult keeping the news quiet, especially from the tenants and villagers. However, she must do her best to contain news of the tragedy, at least until the investigation was well underway. Although she was convinced the vile Benedict Stanton was to blame, until she had proved this was the case it would be better to keep matters quiet. If news leaked out, then it must be that Richard had died in a tragic shooting accident.

She glanced down at her serviceable

promenade gown. By right she should be enveloped in widow's weeds, the house festooned with black ribbons and the shutters closed. Although she had been fond of Richard, she was no more than sad at his passing. Whatever her feelings, she was determined to bring the perpetrators to justice.

On the way to the library, which had now become a study, Emma caught a glimpse of herself in the tall mirror that stood above a side table in the entrance hall. Did she look like a woman who had lost her husband? She stared critically at her appearance — her fair curls still shone with vibrancy, her blue eyes sparkled as usual, and her cheeks were not pale and wan. Her abundant curves demonstrated she was unlikely to go into a decline.

At that moment something she had refused to believe until now shoved its way rudely to the forefront of her mind. She turned away from her reflection in disgust. Richard had been a dear, kind man, always impeccably dressed and good-humoured, but she had not loved him as a true wife should love the man she had married. They had lived in separate apartments. He had visited her to do his duty but a handful of times after that — and if she were honest, she had been relieved when this duty was no longer required of her. She was devastated by his death — of course she was — but her grief was for a friend, not a lover.

Did this make her a heartless woman? She shrugged. It was too late to repine; she had done her duty and been the best wife she could. Now it was time to avenge Richard's untimely death. She vowed she would not rest until his murderer was brought to justice. Whatever it took, whatever she had to do, she would not hesitate, even if it meant sacrificing her good name or giving up her comfortable life.

However, at present there were household matters to attend to. Smithson must prepare a room for the investigator, accommodation must be made for his horse, and she must get ready to receive the lawyers who were due to come later today. She had collected all the documents that related to the estate before she locked the study. There was nothing untoward to be found in them, and she certainly couldn't see how anyone would gain any monetary advantage by murdering Richard. She was at a loss to understand why he had been killed, but she had placed her faith — and a great deal of money — on the experience and expertise of the man coming from Bow Street.

Annie had suggested tactfully that a black gown would be more suitable for the service tomorrow, and Emma had agreed she would wear something sombre — but she was not going to put on black. That would just make things seem worse. She intended to focus on the search for justice and, once that was accomplished, she would be ready to grieve. Only then would she inform her family and put a notice in the *Times*.

Her appetite had all but deserted her;

but as she was of a robust constitution, a few days without eating would do her no harm. The house felt almost normal, as if Richard had just gone away on business as he did so often. The staff must think it odd for Emma to be pretending he was still alive; but they were loyal and well-paid, so she doubted they would complain.

She wandered about the library, pulling out books and pushing them back without any set plan. She was relieved when the butler came to tell her that Mr Dickens, the Stanton family lawyer, was waiting to speak to her.

'Bring him here, please, and have refreshments sent. I believe this could be a long and tedious meeting.'

The butler bowed and left to do her bidding. There was a large leather-topped desk in the bay window, and she decided it would look more business-like if she was seated behind it. There were sufficient chairs placed about the large chamber for the lawyer to find himself one. She should have arranged things before his arrival, but it was too late to do so now. The library door had been left open, and she could hear the lawyer approaching. Hastily she took her place behind the desk, pushed the file of documents to one side of her, and pinned a smile of welcome on her face.

'Mr Dickens, my lady.'

'Come in, Mr Dickens. Bring up a chair and we will get started straight away.'

The lawyer was a man of middle years, medium height and pinched features. He appeared grief-stricken, but Emma did not need his platitudes. Better to stop him before he began to offer his condolences. 'I hope you have followed my instructions and not spoken of my husband's murder to anyone. I have sent for an investigator from Bow Street; and until he is here and has taken charge of matters, I wish no one to know about the tragedy.'

'You are right to be concerned, my lady. I hardly know how to tell you what

I have discovered.'

Emma jerked forward, sending the neatly stacked documents to her left tumbling sideways. Her eyes widened and for a moment she could not reply. She swallowed the bile in her throat and found her voice. 'Tell me at once.'

He fiddled with the papers, gazed round the room for a few seconds and then wiped his eyes. 'There are discrepancies. It would seem that . . . it would seem that someone has had access to Mr Stanton's funds and has, and has . . . ' He couldn't continue, and dropped his head in his hands.

'Are you trying to tell me, sir, that the Stanton investments have been stolen? That somebody in your office is responsible?' Her sharp tone had the desired effect.

'I apologise, my lady, but we are all distraught. Mr Stanton's account has been handled by a senior partner, Mr Chalmers, and it is he who has removed the money. The wretched man has not been into the office this week. We had a note from his wife saying that he was stricken with the summer influenza.'

'Have you informed the magistrate? Are you searching for this man?'

'The theft was only discovered an hour ago, my lady, and we decided it would be better to speak to you before we did anything else. The estates and the income from them remain yours, but everything else has been stolen.'

Emma was on her feet, fury out-weighing her shock. 'You made the right decision, Mr Dickens. I believe I know who is behind this, but I do not wish you to inform the authorities. I shall leave it to the professional to investigate.'

The door at the far end of the room opened and a footman came in with a tray. Emma had no wish for him to see the lawyer, who was sniffling and mumbling into his handkerchief, so she stepped forward and concealed the abject man. 'Put the tray on the side table. We shall serve ourselves. Kindly close the door after you.'

A strong cup of coffee with plenty of sugar should restore Mr Dickens. Cook had sent some dainty almond biscuits and several small slices of plum cake, as well as coffee and drinking chocolate. Keeping her back firmly turned to allow the poor gentleman time to recover his composure, she called out to him: 'Mr Dickens, would you prefer coffee or chocolate to drink?'

The noise of a chair scraping back alerted her. The lawyer was coming to join her. Fortunately there were several comfortable armchairs grouped around the empty fireplace, and a selection of octagonal side tables. They could take their refreshments at this end of the room and then return to the desk when they were both feeling more recovered.

'A cup of coffee, if you please, my lady. I do apologise for — '

'There is no need to apologise; this disaster was not of your making. Now, shall we take our drinks over there and talk of something else until we have finished them?' She gestured to the food and was pleased to see that he put several biscuits and a slice of cake on a plate.

The library had floor-to-ceiling windows at either end, but the other two walls were filled with leather-bound books. As the fireplace was in the centre of one of the book-lined walls, it was a trifle gloomy, but ideal in the circumstances.

They munched and sipped for several minutes without conversing. He was first to break the silence. 'I have been trying to fathom how such a swindle could have taken place without us being aware of it. You will see that all the documents pertaining to the transfer have been signed. It was only on close inspection that we realised the signatures were forgeries. We have no idea how long it took to steal everything; but obviously when the last amount was removed from the accounts, Chalmers fled.'

'Would it be possible to track the money somehow? Surely when stocks and shares are moved from one place to another, there must be a record at the bank.'

'We are looking into that, my lady. But unless we want this matter to become common knowledge, we have to tread carefully. At the moment nobody at the office, apart from myself and my brother, are aware of the enormity of the theft.' He slurped down the last of his coffee and looked hopefully at the tray.

'Would you like me to refill your cup? More biscuits and cake?'

He nodded, his colour now restored, and his appetite too. Once he was settled with his second serving, Emma wandered down to the desk and took her place behind it. Then she reached out and drew the pile of documents he had placed on the desk towards her.

She could see immediately why the fraud had not been discovered until now. The genuine signature was almost indistinguishable from the forgery. Indeed, if she had not been alerted to the problem, she might have missed the fact herself. This Mr Chalmers was not only a thief, but a master forger as well.

The lawyer joined her. 'You will see, my lady, if you peruse from the front to the back of that pile of papers, that the first transfer took place a little over a year ago. As Mr Stanton did not ask us to visit or make enquiries about his holdings, there was no need for either my brother or myself to look into the documents.'

If there had been the slightest doubt in Emma's mind who was behind the swindle and the murder, it now vanished. Mr Stanton had visited just before the time the money started to disappear.

'Is there any way at all that Mr Benedict Stanton can claim Whitford for himself?'

'No, my lady. It is yours. Fortunately your husband appointed Mr Stokes, his man of affairs, to be your trustee and work alongside you. If that were not the case, I can see that there would have been difficulties. However, Mr Stanton would be in a position to take control if you were to die without having remarried.'

Emma's coffee threatened to return. 'How is that possible? I have a will already written, as you know, that leaves everything to my sister and her children.'

'Although the estates are not entailed, my lady, Mr Stanton has an excellent claim in law to keep them in the family. Whitford Hall has been occupied by a Stanton for a century or more, and he could insist that it would be wrong for them to pass to the distaff side.'

'But if I were to be married, this would not be the case? The estates would belong to my husband?'

'That is correct, my lady.'

The meeting was at an end. Emma had no wish to prolong the conversation. She stood and nodded politely; he took the hint and went to gather up the papers.

'I shall need these,' she said. 'Please

leave them with me. No doubt whoever is sent from Bow Street will come and see you in the next day or two.'

She rang the bell and a footman appeared to conduct the lawyer from the premises. As soon as he had left the library, she collapsed into the nearest chair and closed her eyes. Her head was swimming. Her heart was pounding. On her death, Richard's evil brother would get everything. Was her own life in danger too?

3

The ride to Chelmsford took longer than Sam had expected. Even if he had wished to, he could not continue his journey to Whitford Hall today. He decided they would overnight at The Saracen's Head; this was the main posting inn, so it should be a decent place to stay.

They clattered into the yard and he dismounted. 'You see to the horses, Collins, while I see to our accommodation. We'll meet in the common snug — more likely to hear any gossip in there.'

'Right you are, sir. I'm fair famished. I hopes as they have a decent table here.'

Inside the vestibule it was gloomy; insufficient light filtered in through the small leaded panes of the windows. The landlord greeted Sam with a friendly smile. The latter had changed from his normal outfit, which would immediately place him as a Bow Street Runner. Instead he had put on his smart brown riding coat, green waistcoat and freshly starched neckcloth.

'I should like a room for the night; also dinner, when it's ready, for me and my man. He's taken the horses to the stables and will be joining me presently.'

'Certainly, sir. The best rooms are spoken for, but I've a decent chamber at the rear of the property. You will have the room to yourselves; you won't have to share.' He scratched his head and then pointed to a door at the far side of the hall. 'You will have to hurry if you want to eat tonight. The kitchen will be closing in half an hour. Over there, if you're lucky, you'll find yourself a space at a table.' He didn't ask for payment in advance, something that frequently happened when Sam was in his uniform. Not everybody viewed law enforcers as friends.

'I'll stow my bag and then eat,' Sam told him.

The landlord yelled and a potboy in a grubby apron appeared to show Sam to his chamber. The boy didn't bother to open the door for him, just pointed and disappeared. Sam lifted the latch and stepped in, almost braining himself on a beam. Small wonder the boy had been smirking behind his hand.

This room was under the eaves, and he wouldn't be able to stand up without doing himself serious harm: apart from in a small square in the centre of the room, the ceiling was too low. Fortunately the large bed was situated there, but the washstand and commode would require him to approach on his knees if he wished to use them.

The landlord must have realised this chamber was unsuitable for a man as tall as Sam, but he had slept in worse, and at least it was clean. He threw his saddlebag onto the floor and, bending almost double, he removed the pitcher of water and the basin on the stand and placed them carefully on the end of the bed. After a quick wash he was more than ready to find the supper he'd been promised.

Collins had made his way directly to the dining room and claimed two seats at a table. Sam joined him, and immediately a red-faced serving maid plonked a plate of lamb stew and dumplings in front of him.

'This is a bit of all right, sir, and no mistake,' Collins remarked. 'There's ale in the mug — didn't reckon you'd want claret tonight.'

'Thank you, Collins. Are the horses well settled? I warn you, the room we've been given is a death trap. It will be nothing short of miraculous if we manage to get out of it without concussion.' Sam dipped his spoon into the steaming plate and was pleasantly surprised by the flavour. There was freshly baked bread to mop up the juices, and second helpings were freely available.

'That was an excellent meal, Collins,' Sam said when he was done. 'I'm going to join the young bucks and play a hand or two of cards. You go into the public bar and ask a few questions about the family lawyers, Dickens & Dickens.'

★　★　★

When he eventually retired to bed, Sam had gleaned nothing new from his temporary acquaintances. They'd heard of the Stantons, but had nothing bad to say about the family, and had certainly no knowledge of Mr Stanton's untimely demise.

He remembered to duck as he entered his bedchamber, and managed to undress and toss his garments safely to one side before clambering into bed. Collins knew the location of the chamber, had been warned about the beams, and would find his own way to bed when he was ready.

Sam was instantly asleep; the ten years he'd spent as a foot soldier had taught him to take his rest when and where he could. When light spilled into the room he was instantly awake, but not quickly enough to remind his associate to duck.

Collins cracked his head and tumbled to the floor, plunging the room back into darkness. Sam pushed himself up onto one elbow. 'I told you to beware. Serves you right. Stop making that racket; you'll wake the rest of the corridor.'

'Sorry, Sergeant. Bloody hell! Where's the bed? Can't see a bleedin' thing.'

'Shut the door, then four paces and you'll be there. You can stand upright in the middle of the room, but nowhere else. Throw your clothes to the left; mine are on the right. By the by, did you learn anything interesting in the taproom?'

'Nothing at all. Ain't a bad word to be heard about the Stantons nor the lawyers.'

After further muttering and cursing, the bed dipped, and seconds later the room reverberated with the sound of Collins's snoring.

⋆ ⋆ ⋆

Emma arose the following morning with a sense of dread. Whitford Hall no longer felt like her own home, the place she had lived in for the past five years. Perhaps it was because Richard's coffin lay in the family chapel, his death pervading the establishment with sadness.

The vicar was to perform a simple service of committal at midday. The staff, both indoor and out, had leave to attend. Her dresser had put out a sombre dark-brown ensemble, as Emma did not own anything in the correct colour; this was obviously the closest thing that could be found to mourning clothes. The cut was old-fashioned, not having the waistline under the bosom as was favoured currently. The sleeves were long, the neck high and the skirt voluminous. This was not something Emma would choose to wear, especially on such a warm day as this; however, she could hardly appear in her normal attire, as that would appear disrespectful.

Once her hair was plaited and pinned

in a coronet, she was ready to go down and face the day. Stokes was waiting to speak to her. 'There are several business matters to attend to, my lady. Do you wish me to take care of them today?'

'No. I wish to be fully involved with the running of the estates. I have not broken my fast — do you care to join me? Then you can tell me what has to be done.'

He looked somewhat taken aback by her invitation, but half-bowed and nodded. 'If I'm not intruding, I should be delighted to accept. I rarely get the time to breakfast; I have to make do with what I can snatch from the kitchen on my way through.'

She had shared the first meal of the day with Richard, when he was at home, and had been dreading going in today. Having Stokes accompany her was as much for her sake as his. 'I have things I need to share with you as well, Mr Stokes, so this can be our meeting place in future. That way you can be sure of starting the day well fed, and I do not have to sit in here on my own.'

There was no need to offer further explanation; he understood immediately. 'Thank you, my lady. There will not always be business to discuss, but I think it wise to keep each other informed of what is going on.'

Once they were seated — he with a piled plate, she with toast and butter — she told him what Mr Dickens had said the previous day.

'The master had no time for his brother, my lady. He thought him a thoroughly bad lot. He has set up things so that it will be impossible for Mr Stanton to interfere with the running of the estates and farms.'

'My husband could only do that because we both trust you implicitly, Mr Stokes. I can still hardly credit that the senior partner at Dickens & Dickens has stolen everything. Will we be able to manage this quarter without the added income?'

'It will be tight going, my lady, but we'll come about somehow. If you please, I wish to speak to you about keeping the death of the master secret, as I fear that won't be possible. The village and farms are used to seeing him on a regular basis, and if he doesn't make his usual rounds they'll soon realise something's not right.'

Emma's eyes filled. He was correct, of course: it was stupid to think Richard's death could be hidden. She swallowed the lump in her throat. 'I agree, Mr Stokes, but I do not wish to make any announcement until after I have spoken to the investigator. He should be arriving this morning.'

'We will have to give the staff black armbands to wear once the news is out. Shall I put the matter in hand?'

'I shall speak to the housekeeper. There is bound to be some suitable material she can have made up.' As she had been speaking, Emma had come to a surprising decision. 'I shall be moving to London, Mr Stokes. I shall be incommunicado whilst I'm gone, and will rely on you to run things efficiently in my absence. I believe there is more likelihood of apprehending the perpetrators of the murder and the theft in Town.'

'I understand your wish to seek justice for the master, but — '

'Mr Stokes, might I remind you that although you are ostensibly in charge of Whitford Hall, that is merely a facade. What I choose to do is entirely my concern.'

If he was shocked by her sharp reply, he did not show it. His kindly blue eyes glittered as he answered quietly. 'I hope you'll take your maid and a groom with you. You cannot wander about the city unprotected.'

Somewhat ashamed of her outburst, Emma smiled. 'I shall indeed, Mr Stokes, and I thank you for your concern. As there are no funds available, I shall take my jewellery and sell that when I am there. I have sufficient money to be able to rent some modest accommodation. I have no intention of appearing anywhere I might be recognised.'

'Forgive me for asking, my lady, but

what exactly do you hope to achieve by masquerading as a common person?'

She had scarcely worked out the details for herself, as this had been a sudden decision. 'Mr Stanton has never met me. I intend to become acquainted with him, and by so doing uncover his perfidy and bring him to justice.'

Stokes looked dubious. 'The master wouldn't want you to put yourself in any danger, my lady, though it's not my place to comment. Anything you require me to do, just send word.'

★　★　★

Emma returned to the library and positioned herself so she could see anyone arriving. Her man of business had only been gone a short while when a tall man, riding a large dun gelding, cantered into view. He was accompanied by another man, and both looked tough and efficient. Hastily, she removed herself from the window; it would not do to be seen gawping like a child.

Bentley, the butler, already had his instructions and would conduct the visitor to the library immediately when he arrived. The man, who was obviously the senior investigator, had dark hair worn unfashionably long, and broad shoulders to match his height. His clothes were smart but not elegant. Her brother-in-law was a large man, but his bulk was due to indulgence, whereas the man she had just observed looked anything but flabby.

Emma decided to seat herself behind the desk where she had sat when speaking to the lawyer, as she had no wish to be intimidated by either man's size. Richard had been slender and not above average height, but for all that he had been an excellent rider and able to stay out all day with the hunt and return scarcely out of breath.

Belatedly, she thought, perhaps it might have been wise to have arranged for her maid to sit discreetly in the library so she was chaperoned. But no — that rule only applied to innocents;

and anyway, protecting her reputation was no longer of any interest to her.

A further quarter of an hour ticked by before the visitor was announced. 'Sergeant Ross, my lady — senior investigator from Bow Street.'

Bentley stepped aside; and if she had not been seated, Emma feared her legs might have given way beneath her. Nothing had prepared her for the impact this stranger had on her. Although he was clean-shaven, she could see dark stubble on his cheeks. His jaw was firm and his complexion sun-darkened, but it was his eyes that held her attention. They were as dark as his hair, and she was held firm by their intensity.

He bowed and she was able to breathe again. 'I bid you good morning, my lady. I'm Sergeant Ross. Constable Collins is taking care of our mounts. He won't require indoor accommodation.'

'I am pleased to see you, Sergeant. I have had the study locked since my husband died. I shall take you there immediately.'

Whatever Sam had been expecting, it had not been to see a widow who looked scarcely old enough to have been a wife. She was as fair as he was dark, and her sky-blue eyes held him captive. She was the most beautiful woman he'd ever seen. Working with her was going to be a downright pleasure.

He received a second shock when she emerged from behind the desk. She was far taller than he'd realised, and her form was rounded in all the right places. He had the devil of a job to keep his appreciation from showing on his face. Her husband had been murdered yesterday — was not yet buried; and yet she was not dressed in black and didn't seem unduly miserable. Did this mean the marriage had been unhappy? The letter that she had sent to Mr Fletcher hadn't given any details; it merely offered a substantial sum and requested that the best investigator should come immediately to discover who had murdered Mr Stanton.

By the time she'd explained the circumstances of the death, told him about the theft of the family investments, and said she suspected her brother-in-law, Sam was convinced this was a case that would require all his investigative powers. There was nothing he liked better than getting his teeth into a juicy murder; and having a beautiful widow as his employer would make things even more interesting.

'This is the study,' she said as they arrived outside the door. 'I hope you don't mind if I don't accompany you. I should find it too distressing.'

'It's not necessary for you to come in, my lady. Collins and I will give the place a thorough search. There's only one explanation — there must be a secret passage. Did your husband ever mention this to you?'

'Of course; how stupid of me. It is the only explanation that makes sense. I have never heard of such a thing, but I will send my butler to you. He has worked here all his life. If anyone knows about a secret passage, it will be him.' She unlocked the door and walked away, her bearing upright, and her movements graceful despite her height and size.

Collins arrived at the same time as the butler. 'I believe that I know where to find the passageway you are seeking, Sergeant Ross,' said the latter. 'Although I have never seen it, I do recall there was talk of such a thing many years ago. I believe it to have been something to do with the hiding of Catholic priests. The Stantons were once of the old faith.'

The study was much as one would have expected in a house of this size. There was a bureau, a substantial desk, several filled bookcases, and a group of chairs and a side table at the far end of the room under the window for more informal discussions. A large, elaborately carved fireplace was in the centre of the outside wall, and it was to this the butler hurried. Sam and Collins joined him, and soon they were all twisting and pressing the various protuberances.

'Dammit to hell!' Sam muttered in annoyance. 'The fireplace is obviously not going to reveal its secret. Are you quite sure, Bentley, that this is where we should be looking?'

The elderly black-garbed gentleman shook his head in bewilderment. 'I am sure when I was a boot boy that I overheard a conversation between a footman and a parlourmaid, and they said that one opened the secret door in the study by pressing the centre of a wooden flower.'

Sam stepped away from the fireplace in order to examine the rest of the room. At first he saw nothing of interest; but then halfway between the two bookcases he saw an ancient carving of a Norman keep. He strode across and examined the panel. Sure enough, there was an area in the centre of the tower that looked slightly shinier than the rest. Could this be what they were looking for?

He reached out and jammed the heel of his hand against the spot, and immediately there was the rumbling noise. The panel rolled aside, revealing a pitch-dark opening that could only be the secret passageway through which the murderer had arrived and departed.

4

'Collins, find yourself a lantern and explore this passageway,' Sam said. 'I need to speak to Lady Emma immediately.' He was relieved the study door had remained locked, for he was now convinced her life could well be in danger. 'See where this comes out, and then we must ensure it can no longer be used.'

He went in search of his employer. As soon as the committal service was over, he would suggest she take a prolonged visit to family or friends until he had apprehended those involved in this crime. For her to be called Lady Emma, she must be the daughter of an earl at the very least — she would be safe enough in her familial home.

His quarry was in the library, looking through a pile of documents. 'We have found the secret passage, my lady,' he informed her. 'My man is investigating it at the moment.'

'I am glad you have discovered how the murderer was able to get in and out of the house without being seen. Sergeant Ross, I neglected to tell you that my husband had received a letter from London the morning he was killed. I found no trace of it in the study, so the murderer must have taken it with him.'

'The more I hear about this case, the more sure I am that Mr Stanton is behind it. You're not safe here, my lady; you must leave immediately and make a prolonged visit to your family.'

'I have every intention of leaving here when you do, Sergeant — not to go to visit friends or family, but to accompany you to London.'

Sam listened with growing incredulity to her plans. 'I will not allow it, my lady — '

'It is immaterial to me, Sergeant, how you feel about the matter. I employ you, not the other way round. My mind is quite made up. I shall be perfectly safe, as my brother-in-law has never met me, and I have not been about in society since I had my come-out six years ago.'

'I think it's the height of folly, my lady. What is more, my job is to track down and apprehend perpetrators, not to play bodyguard to you.'

'I understand, sir, and will not get in the way of your investigation. However, I am sure that if we worked together, we would achieve our objective more quickly.'

Sam was unused to being given orders by a woman. He was damned if he was going to be dictated to, even by someone as lovely as Lady Emma. Then he thought of a way he could prevent her from accompanying him. 'I agree, but in order for this deception to work we must masquerade as husband and wife. That way I can remain under your roof and keep you safe, and we can attend functions together without causing comment.'

He had expected her to recoil; to throw her aristocratic hands in the air and send him packing. Instead, she smiled — the first time she had done so since he had met her that morning — and he was lost.

'I should have thought of that myself, Sergeant Ross. We must invent a suitable name and decide where we shall rent a house. Is there any danger that you will be recognised?'

For a moment he was unable to respond; his composure was in tatters. Then he swallowed and cleared his throat. 'I do not move in even the lower levels of society, my lady, so nobody will know me.'

'Good. Forgive me for asking, but do you have a more extensive wardrobe at your London home? Although we shall not be mixing with the *ton*, you will require something with more elegance if you are not to be found out at once.'

No sooner were the words out of her mouth than Emma regretted her remark. Sam's lips thinned and his eyes flashed dangerously. She had offended him.

'I am a Bow Street Runner, my lady.

I live in rented rooms and I am wearing my only respectable garments. If these do not pass muster, then so be it. The choice is yours. Take me as I am, or forget about it and leave me to get on with my job unhampered by an unwanted female.'

'I beg your pardon, sir. I spoke without thought.' He did not seem inclined to accept her apology, so what she was about to say might make matters even worse. 'There is a closet full of unwanted garments upstairs. They belonged to my father-in-law, who was of a similar height and build to you. Although they will be a trifle outdated, they were made at Weston's and would be ideal.'

A dark flush spread along Sam's cheekbones and she was sure she heard his teeth grinding. She braced herself for the onslaught of invective, but he held on to his temper and the danger passed.

'I too shall be in disguise,' she told him. 'My dresser is at this very moment finding me gowns that will be suitable for my new persona. Please do not scowl at me, Sergeant — you know what I am saying makes sense.'

He nodded briefly. 'Very well, I will select something this evening. I shall leave at first light tomorrow and go on ahead to find a suitable property. Tavistock Place would be ideal for our purposes; it's smart but not grand. I shall send word here as soon as I have located something. You must be ready to leave at a moment's notice.'

'I shall give you my jewellery to sell. I'm sure that you will get a better price for it than I would. We will also need funds; and as you know, there are none in any of my accounts until the next quarter's rents are paid.'

For some reason this suggestion caused further upset between them, and his scowl returned. 'That won't be necessary, my lady. You've already given me more than enough to take care of our expenses.'

'Good. However, I shall take my jewellery in case we have need of extra.

It might take several weeks to achieve our objective.'

He ignored her comment. 'Often rented premises come with staff, but I think it would be better if you bring your own people as well,' he advised her. 'A groom, stable lad and coachman, plus a cook, two parlourmaids and your dresser should suffice. I noticed there is an antiquated carriage in the coach house; you must use that. I shall select the team to pull it and the men who will accompany us.'

It was her turn to bristle. He was taking too much upon himself, and issuing orders as if she were in some way under his control. She had no wish to continue this conversation and stood up abruptly. 'In which case, sir, I shall leave you to your enquiries. My husband's service is at noon. I would appreciate it if you would attend.'

'I should be honoured, my lady.' He bowed and marched out.

Sam's bearing, manners and demeanour were those of a soldier and not a gentleman. Emma knew she must resign herself to spending time with someone from the lower orders, and must not expect him to behave as Richard would have done. She bit her lip and swallowed an unwanted lump in her throat. For her husband's sake, she must be strong. She would not dwell on her loss until his murder was avenged and the money stolen from the estates had been returned.

★　★　★

The service was mercifully brief, and Richard's coffin was placed with suitable reverence in the family crypt. There had been a space prepared for him and he was lowered in. Emma had no wish to wait and see the marble slabs placed across the grave. His inscription was already carved; even the date of his death. All the staff had come to the simple service in the family chapel; but only Mr Stokes, Sergeant Ross and the vicar had accompanied

Emma into the cold and dark interior of the underground crypt in which generations of Stantons had been interred. The heavy door was closed behind them as she emerged, blinking, into the bright sunlight. Richard was the last — she would not allow her brother-in-law a place in the family vault.

She turned to Mr Stokes, who was hovering solicitously beside her. 'Have the door bricked up,' she told him. 'I have no wish to ever go down there again, and there are no more members of this family to join my husband and his ancestors.'

'I shall have it done today, my lady. I think you are right to do this. When are you leaving for London?'

'Sergeant Ross leaves at first light tomorrow, but I shall not depart until I get word from him that he has secured us a suitable property. Whilst I am away, you must refrain from contacting me unless it is an emergency. I am relying on you to run Whitford Hall and the estates in my absence. Deal with any complaints or problems as you see fit — I trust your judgement implicitly.'

He nodded and left her side to arrange for the workmen to permanently seal the door to the family vault. Sergeant Ross took the vacant place at her side. 'I offer my condolences for your tragic loss, my lady. I give you my word that I will bring the perpetrator to justice so that you may return here and live in safety.'

She wiped her eyes with her handkerchief. 'I thank you, Sergeant. It is a very sad day indeed. However, I shall put my grief and widow's weeds aside until Benedict Stanton receives his just deserts.'

They walked in silence to the house, and she was strangely comforted by having Sam's solid presence close by. He might not be a member of her social class, or a gentleman born, but he was an honest and steady man, which was exactly what she required at the moment.

'We shall dine at five o'clock, sir. There is no need to dress. I have had all the garments that are suitable taken to your bedchamber. My husband's valet, Benton, will attend to you now. It will be expected of you. As far as the resident staff are concerned, we are a well-to-do couple moving temporarily to the city for business reasons. They cannot suspect for a moment we are not what we say we are.'

'I suppose that makes sense, my lady,' Sam replied. 'There are still many details we need to discuss, but that can wait until dinner. By the by, Collins has found sufficient evidence at the end of the tunnel to confirm our suspicions. The bricklayers can close the exit to the secret passageway after they have completed their work over there.'

'It will be a relief to know that nobody else can get into the house undetected. Mr Stokes will be living here in my absence. He is a distant relative of the Stantons and is totally honest and loyal to the family.'

Sam looked unconvinced. 'A week ago you would have said that about the legal crow who has taken all your money. You might have no redress if he refuses to relinquish his control when you return. Are you quite certain you wish to take that risk?'

'My husband would not have arranged matters as they are if he did not trust Mr Stokes implicitly. Anyway, I have always the legal right to reside here, regardless of who is running the estates. Of course, if I marry at any point, control will immediately go to my new husband.'

What had possessed her to mention marriage? He was her employee, not a member of her family, and she would do better not to talk to him so informally. Before he could respond, she bid him a curt 'good day' and hurried away. She was almost running when she reached the side door they had used earlier.

★   ★   ★

Sam watched her go with a wry smile. The next few weeks were going to be interesting to say the least. He veered off towards the stables, where Collins had been inspecting the horses and the men.

'Sergeant, I reckon these two nags would be ideal — solid horseflesh but no thoroughbreds. It seems her ladyship likes to ride. You taking her gelding with you?'

'I think not. The area I am intending to rent a house in is some distance from the nearest park, so Lady Emma will have to do without a riding horse whilst we are in London. As it is, we're going to require a substantial property, as we will have a carriage, two riding horses and the team to find room for. Stabling and fodder is exorbitant in the city — I just hope this investigation doesn't take too long or I'll run out of blunt.'

Having arranged matters satisfactorily for his departure tomorrow, Sam went to speak to Stokes. He just hoped her ladyship's faith in this man was not misplaced. She was right to say that only by remarrying would her position and property be safe. Why did this prospect make him angry? He was a common man, she an aristocrat, and what she did with her life was no business of his.

He lashed out at the wooden pail standing by the archway, and it flew into the air, emptying its contents on his breeches. He turned the air blue and heard a stable boy sniggering behind him. He spun, but the offending youth had mysteriously vanished.

Sam was forced to smile at his foolishness. He deserved to be soaked to the skin for behaving like a spoilt brat. There was no option but to return to the house, find his chamber and change his raiment. He paused at the side door through which Lady Emma had disappeared to remove his boots and empty them of water. In his stockinged feet, he padded through the house until he discovered a footman who could escort him to his quarters, whereby he pushed open the door to find himself in a well-appointed sitting room. This chamber alone was bigger than his entire apartment. His arrival attracted the attention of a small middle-aged man dressed impeccably in black.

'Good afternoon, Sergeant Ross. I am Benton, at your service. If you would care to hand me your boots, I will get them dry and returned to you directly. If you would care to take a bath, I can have water brought up immediately.'

For a moment Sam thought the man was being impertinent, suggesting that he smelt unsavoury. Then he realised Benton was merely doing his best to be of service to him. 'A bath would be splendid, but not if it will put the kitchen under pressure providing water at this time of day.'

'It will be no trouble at all, sir; and whilst you are bathing I can restore your boots so they are clean and dry when you need them.'

In a remarkably short time Sam was

relaxing in lemon-scented water in a small room that was set aside purely for the purpose of ablutions. He could not help smiling. When he had left Bow Street yesterday he had been an ordinary fellow, and here he was transformed into a gentleman.

His new man had the sense to keep out of his way whilst he was in the bath, but had left soft white towels waiting on a rack for when he wished to step out and dry himself. Sam wallowed in the water until it was almost tepid. He could not remember the last time he had had the luxury of a bath. He kept clean by the same method most people used, if they bothered to keep clean at all — a strip wash; but in future he would take a bath whenever the opportunity presented itself.

Reluctantly, Sam eventually stood up and stepped onto the mat, then reached out to remove one of the large towels. There was a full-length mirror attached to the wall opposite, and he paused before wrapping himself in the towel to examine his naked body. This was something else he had not been able to do before, as he had only a small cracked glass in which to view himself when he shaved.

He ran his fingers thoughtfully over the scar that ran across his belly. He had been lucky to survive that wound — it had put him out of action for several months, and only the skill of the field doctor had saved his life. There were half a dozen other scars received at various points during his long career, though none had been life-threatening; more an inconvenience than anything else.

Still gazing with interest into the mirror, he decided he was still in decent shape for a man of two-and-thirty. His muscles were still hard. No sign of flab around the middle, thank the good Lord. He had been soldiering his entire adult life and knew no other trade. If he were to retain his position as a senior investigator for Mr Fletcher, he had to remain fit.

Sam dried himself, and with a clean towel around his middle wandered into the adjacent dressing room, where he found that his new valet had laid out a selection of jackets and waistcoats for him to look at, as well as shirts, stockings and neckcloths. The man himself was absent — whether from design or accident, he'd no idea; but Sam was more comfortable dressing himself. He was prepared to tolerate a personal servant as long as he did not intrude on his privacy.

Sam shrugged into a fine lawn shirt, far better than anything he'd ever worn before, then tucked the tails between his legs and pulled on a pair of buff breeches. They fitted remarkably well: a trifle loose at the waist, but not too short in the leg, which was surprising as he stood over two yards high in his stockinged feet. Then he quickly buttoned the front flap of his breeches and pulled on a pair of silk stockings, relieved to find that his dry, polished boots were waiting for him.

He was looking through the waistcoats and jackets when Benton reappeared. Without being asked, the man picked up a brown and black striped waistcoat and held it out for him. He must suppose this man knew his business, because it was the last one he would have chosen for himself. Then Benton helped him into a dark-brown worsted coat that fitted well enough.

'If you would care to be seated, sir, I shall arrange your hair and tie your cravat.'

Sam was about to protest, to tell the man he was quite capable of doing both for himself, but something stopped him. If he was to pretend to be a gentleman, then he had better learn damn quickly what was involved. When his valet had done, Sergeant Ross appeared to have vanished, and a stranger stared back at him.

5

Emma wished she had not agreed to dine with Sergeant Ross. She was overwhelmed with sadness at the loss of her partner, and even her anger and determination to bring the perpetrators to justice were not enough to revive her spirits. Now she regretted her impulse to employ a Bow Street Runner, and to remove herself from all that she held dear to go and live in London. She was an unnatural woman. Didn't she owe Richard more than a few tears shed in private?

But she had not the energy to change. It hardly mattered what she wore to eat with the sergeant; it was scarcely his place to notice. If she had thought of it, she would have asked Mr Stokes to join them. After all, he was in charge of the estates, and a gentleman born. It was too late to do so now, however, and she must go down and join her guest. He was right to say there was much to discuss if they were to be successful in their masquerade.

Cook had been instructed to serve a simple meal, no removes and just three courses. Emma walked straight to the dining room without detouring into the drawing room, where she and Richard had always met for a glass of wine before dining.

Bentley had had the good sense to serve the meal in a chamber that had never been used to dine in — it would be far easier sitting somewhere fresh. Presumably Sergeant Ross would be directed to this room when he came down. She wandered to the window and stared morosely out onto the acres of rolling parkland that surrounded the house. The formal gardens were on the east and west of the building; the north was where the turning circle and front door were positioned; and the south (where Emma was standing now) faced the park in which deer grazed in order to keep the grass neat.

'I apologise if I have kept you waiting, my lady, but I've been standing in the drawing room this past quarter of an hour.'

Sergeant Ross had joined her, and he sounded no more overjoyed at the prospect of dining together than she was. Slowly she turned to face him, and her eyes widened. She scarcely recognised the tall gentleman who stood before her in his borrowed finery. If she had not known him to be a rough soldier, then she would have thought him a member of society. 'I am sorry,' she said. 'Bentley should have directed you here. I see that my father-in-law's clothes are an excellent fit.' She regretted her comment as soon as she had spoken. It was hardly polite to remind him he was beholden to her.

Instead of being offended, he smiled, and she was reminded again that he was very handsome. 'I'm a new man, my lady, and I'm looking forward to playing the part of a person well above my station.' His dry tone made it clear he did not in any way feel himself inferior to her despite his lowly origins.

A footman glided forward and held out a chair for Emma, and once she was seated he did the same for her guest. They sat in silence whilst a leek and potato soup was served and freshly baked rolls and butter were placed between them. When she had asked for a simple meal, Emma had not expected something quite so rustic, and for a moment was afraid Sam would think he was being patronised. However, he dipped into his bowl with obvious enjoyment, and after a few tentative sips she discovered her own appetite had returned. They both had a second helping, and when the main course was brought in, Emma was ready to do it justice.

They were left alone to eat, and when they had both cleared their plates, Sam wiped his mouth on his napkin and dropped it onto his empty plate. Whatever his background, his table manners were impeccable, and for that she was grateful.

'Lady Emma, have you decided what we shall be called? We must get the details clear before we embark on this extraordinary venture.'

'Obviously I can no longer use my title, but apart from that I have not thought much about it. I think it best to stick to our given names, but I have no notion as to what our second name should be.'

'I know that you're Emma, I'm Samuel, but called Sam by my friends. I think it best if we don't settle on a name that's linked in any way to either of us.'

He leaned back in his chair and closed his eyes, giving Emma a moment to study him. The hard planes of his face, which was immaculately clean-shaven, made him stand out as a man of strength and character. And now that his hair had been tamed and tied back in an old-fashioned queue at the nape of his neck, no one would doubt that he was a gentleman. Perhaps not one at the forefront of fashion, but a gentleman nonetheless.

'Ashfield — Mr and Mrs Ashfield,' he said. 'We're in Town because of my business interests in the city, but have a neat estate in Suffolk or some such place. Too far to be driving back and forth each day, hence the need to rent a house for a few months.'

'I like it,' Emma said with a smile. 'Whilst I am Mrs Emma Ashfield I can put aside this life, pretend that my husband did not die so suddenly, and concentrate on priorities. We shall have to inform the staff who will be going with us, but they are loyal and will not betray us.'

'Have you any thoughts about how you're going to insinuate yourself into Mr Stanton's circle of friends?' Sam asked her. 'You need to tell me what you know about him, and how he and your husband came to be estranged.'

Bentley came in with two footmen, and they cleared the table before setting an array of desserts between the two diners and vanishing again. The wine had been left within reach, and Sam had been keeping their glasses topped up.

'My husband was the only child of my father-in-law's first marriage,' Emma began. 'He never knew his mama, for she died in childbirth. His father married again three years later, and Benedict Stanton was born. Naturally his own mama favoured him, and Richard was his father's favourite. This set up an intense rivalry that came to a head when the second Mrs Stanton died. Benedict insisted he should have equal rights over the estate — that it should be split between them, but Mr Stanton refused. He settled a substantial annuity on his second son, but the family properties remained with Richard.' She paused, unable to continue.

'Do not carry on with your story, my lady, if it upsets you.'

'No, I am able to finish this sorry tale. The bitterness came from Benedict;

79

Richard made every effort to repair the rift, but to no avail. When we married five years ago, his brother had moved to London and was living a rackety life, and his father had died.'

'Something must have changed for Stanton to murder your husband. From what you have said, it might well be that his fortune has gone, and the only way he can retrench is by stealing from his brother. You mentioned the missing letter as well; I imagine they must have been informing your husband of the theft, and that somehow Benedict Stanton got wind of this and sent a man to recover them.'

Emma wished she had not eaten so much, as her meal threatened to return. 'Are you saying that my husband's death might have been unintentional? That the murderer came to collect the incriminating letter, but finding Richard in the study, was forced to kill him?'

He nodded, his expression grim. 'It makes no sense otherwise, my lady. Stanton had already purloined thousands of pounds, more than enough to keep him comfortable for the remainder of his life if he so wished. Why should he risk everything by killing your husband and setting up a hue and cry?'

'But Mr Stokes thought Richard had killed himself — the pistol was in his hand. If I had not heard someone in the study, I might eventually have believed this to be the case, especially when I learned that we were all but ruined.'

Emma's head was awash with possibilities, and none of them pleasant. Then something occurred to her that contradicted what Sam had just said. 'The letter Richard received had come from London. But the lawyers in Chelmsford did not know that the money had been stolen until I contacted them yesterday, so the correspondence must have been about something else.'

Sam thumped the table, making the remaining cutlery and crystalware jump. 'Dammit to hell! I'm supposed to be an investigator — I should have thought of this for myself. If the letters were not about the missing money, then they had to contain something incriminating about your brother-in-law. Can you think of any business acquaintance of your husband's who might have had knowledge of Mr Benedict Stanton's criminal intentions?'

'Sergeant Ross, if we are to deal well together over the next few weeks, I must ask you to refrain from using bad language in my presence. It is not something I am used to and I find it offensive.'

Sam stared at her as if she were speaking in tongues, and then tossed back the last of his claret and pushed himself upright. Only then did Emma realise he was a trifle bosky, had consumed the best part of two bottles of wine over dinner.

'I beg your pardon, my lady, if my manners are not up to your high standards. As I told you before, I'm no more than a rough soldier, and you cannot make a silk purse out of a sow's ear.'

There was no answer to that, and she

let him leave the room without comment. Up until that point she had been relaxed in his company; had almost forgotten he wasn't from her stratum of society. Richard had always been gently spoken; during the years they had been together she had never known him to raise his voice. Indeed, when she came to think of it, not only had he never raised his voice, but he had also agreed with everything she said.

She wiped her eyes on her napkin as his dear face filled her thoughts. She was going to miss him dreadfully — not, if she were honest, as a husband, but as a friend. It was hardly surprising they had not been blessed with children, as he had not visited her bedroom since the early days of their marriage. A slight shiver ran down her spine as she recalled that not only had Richard not been interested in bedroom matters, but he had never kissed her on the lips and had rarely even touched her. Why had he married her if he had not found her desirable? This lack of physical contact had not bothered her until she had met Sergeant Ross.

She was unable to move as things that she had pushed to the back of her mind finally made sense. Her relationship with Richard had been that of siblings living together, not as a husband and wife should live. He must have married her to run his house, because he had certainly shown no interest in filling his nursery; neither had he wanted her as his hostess, for they had never entertained.

There was still a glass of wine left in the decanter, and Emma filled her glass. She was not in the habit of imbibing alcohol, but after the last two days of tragedy and revelation she needed to steady her nerves. Possibly brandy would be better, but she had no intention of calling for a footman, so the remains of the claret would have to do.

Her marriage had been one of expedience for both of them. She had chosen Richard because he was intelligent, attractive in a quiet sort of way, and undemanding, and he had made her an offer for the same reason. Her father had been a domineering parent, and she had learnt to hold her tongue and do as she was told, as her mother and sisters did. Only her younger brother was exempt from the tongue-lashings and beatings they all suffered at the earl's hands.

Richard had offered her a sanctuary and had been prepared to marry her without her dowry. He had never made her heart skip a beat, and neither had she missed him when he was away on his frequent business trips. After five years of being her own mistress, making decisions and living as she pleased, Emma believed her true character had eventually emerged. She was not a quiet mouse of a woman, but a strong and determined person who was more than ready to seek revenge for her husband's death. He had made no demands on her in his lifetime, so she would do this one last thing for him before she got on with her own life.

Mr Dickens had said it would make sense for her to marry, as the estates would not then go her to brother-in-law on her demise. Next time she took a step into matrimony, she would do so only if her feelings were engaged. Whitford Hall must start a new life, and no longer be the ancestral home of the Stanton family, because one thing she was very certain of was that Benedict Stanton would never get his hands on it, even though he was the last of the line.

* ★ ★ ★

Sam woke with a head like a bear pit, and a temper to match. He was not a big drinker, preferring to stick to ale, and should never have had so much of that fancy red wine last night. He had behaved like a buffoon, and owed his employer an apology, but that would have to wait until she came to London and moved into the house he had yet to rent for them.

He rolled out of bed, forgetting he had a valet to take care of him now, and headed for the washroom. After his ablutions and a quick shave, he found a clean shirt and stockings, but put on the same jacket and breeches he had been wearing the day before. The only thing he possessed of any value was his pocket watch, which had been given to him by Wellington himself, and he treasured it. He flicked open the silver case and saw the time was a little after four o'clock. After ramming a few things into his saddlebags, he was ready to go. He would leave the packing of everything else to his valet, as he had no time to waste on such trivialities.

Downstairs was dark, as the sconces had burnt out, but there was sufficient dawn light filtering through the shutters to enable him to find his way to the side door. Collins would be ready, his horse would be saddled, and they could stop to rest the horses and breakfast at Romford.

'Mornin', sir, and a fine one it is too.'

His constable gestured towards two young men neatly dressed in buff breeches and topcoats. 'These two are coming with us. One of them will come back with the address when we have it. They both know what's what, if you know what I mean.'

'Good enough. From now on I am Samuel Ashfield, Esquire, a well-to-do businessman visiting London for a few weeks. Make sure they know to refer to me as such in future, and to refer to her ladyship as Mrs Ashfield.'

Collins touched his cap and ambled across to speak to the two waiting grooms. Whilst he was doing so, Sam mounted and set off. They could catch him up, but he needed to gallop the cobwebs from his drink-befuddled brain.

They made good time and arrived in the city by mid-morning. Sam headed for the offices of a lawyer he knew to deal in the renting and purchasing of property. He had not met him himself, but had heard his name spoken in Bow

Street once or twice.

Collins and the grooms waited outside with the horses whilst he went in. Despite his slightly dishevelled appearance — spending several hours in the saddle was not conducive to a smart exterior — he was bowed and scraped into the presence of a senior partner. He explained his requirements while the man nodded and smiled.

'I have exactly the property you need, Mr Ashfield. It is recently vacated, as the owners have returned to the country to take care of an ailing parent. It is fully furnished to the highest order and has a number of experienced staff to run it.'

'It needs to have stabling, a coach house and accommodation for my grooms. And as my wife is not fond of the city, there must be a decent garden for her to walk in. We are bringing half a dozen of our most loyal staff with us, but I'm happy to keep on those who are already there. I am hoping to complete my business in Town within a couple of months, but it could be longer. Would this be satisfactory for the owners?'

The lawyer nodded and smiled some more. 'Perfectly, Mr Ashfield, perfectly. Here are the particulars, and the costs involved.'

Sam glanced at the paper and was shocked to see how expensive the rent was, but he hid his dismay well. He had sufficient funds to cover the first few weeks, but Lady Emma's jewellery would have to go if they didn't complete their task speedily. 'That will be agreeable. Do you require a deposit? I have a bank draft here.'

Half an hour later Sam left with the keys to the property in his hand. He had scribbled down the directions and address and handed this to one of the grooms, to whom he said: 'Your horse is tired. Stop at Romford for refreshments and let the beast eat and rest before continuing. You should be at your destination before dark. Accompany Mrs Ashfield when she sets off tomorrow.' The groom touched his whip to his cap, tucked the paper inside his jacket and clattered off down the street.

'Right, let's go and see this house and get ourselves settled,' Sam said. He was finding it hard not to whistle. He was going to enjoy being a gentleman and living in the lap of luxury at somebody else's expense for a few weeks. Having the delectable Lady Emma as his companion would be no hardship either.

6

The journey into London gave Emma sufficient time to adjust to her new personality. She was travelling with her abigail in a somewhat dilapidated carriage that had been resurrected from the coach house. The under-cook, a footman, Sam's valet and two maids had set off at dawn and were travelling by public stagecoach. The trunks and other paraphernalia were strapped to the back of Emma's carriage.

'Annie, I think you must practise calling me 'madam' or 'Mrs Ashfield'. It would not do for you to slip up and use my real name once we are settled in our new abode.' They were entering the outskirts of the city and Emma looked out of the window with interest. 'It seems years since I was in Town for my debut, and I can scarcely remember it at all. We shall be living in Tavistock

Place, which I understand to be in a reasonable part of London, although not quite as grand as Grosvenor Square where my father has a property.'

'I've never been to London, Mrs Ashfield, and I can tell you I'm excited to be here despite the noxious smells and smoke.'

'I shall endeavour to see that you get some free time so you can explore the sights. I shall certainly make my way to Bond Street, and I wish to see the animals at the Tower of London. June is not a fashionable time to be here, which is fortunate as I have no wish to be recognised when I am out.'

'If you keep your bonnet on, madam, I reckon you'll go unnoticed in the crowds. Nobody could forget you once they have seen your beautiful hair — I doubt there are many other young ladies with hair the colour of sunshine.'

'Perhaps I should stain it with walnut juice just to be sure.'

'I hope you will not do any such thing, Mrs Ashfield. It would be a shame to spoil the beauty of it.'

The carriage rocked violently, tipping them both from the seat into the well of the carriage. By the time they had picked themselves up, the coachman had shouted down his apologies and Emma had forgotten the discussion about her locks.

It took an unconscionable time to wend their way through the narrow streets until they reached the more salubrious area to the west of the city. Emma gazed out of the window like a country bumpkin, fascinated by all she saw, and Annie also had her nose pressed to the glass on the other side of the vehicle. They passed Lincoln's Inn Fields and the Foundling Hospital, then turned down a wide street. This was a residential area with fewer pedestrians and carriages to hold them up.

'Is my bonnet straight, Annie? Is my face free of smuts and grime? I must make a good impression, for I am certain the wife of a prosperous businessman would always wish to look her best.'

'You look very smart, madam. Your bonnet hasn't moved since I adjusted it for you after we fell off the seat a while ago.'

The carriage turned left and right, then pulled up outside a modern property. Their arrival had been seen from the house, as the front door opened and the young footman from Whitford Hall hurried down to open the door and let down the steps. He offered Emma his hand and she stepped out, waiting to see how she would be addressed. However, the footman didn't speak, but merely bowed and escorted her to the front door where the resident butler and housekeeper were waiting.

'Welcome to Tavistock Place, madam. I am the butler here, Foster, and this is the housekeeper, Mrs Philips. The luggage arrived safely earlier today and your apartment is ready.'

By this time they were inside the

property, and Emma looked around with surprise. The floor had smart black and white tiles, the walls were fashionably striped in green and gold, and light poured in from the two large windows on either side of the front door. Even the furniture and appointments were elegant.

'Thank you, Foster. I am pleasantly surprised. Is Mr Ashfield home at present?'

'No, madam, but he will be back for dinner.'

The housekeeper stepped forward and curtsied. She was a surprisingly young woman, no more than thirty years of age at the most, with a pleasing countenance and friendly smile. 'If you would care to come this way, Mrs Ashfield, I'll conduct you to your rooms.'

Emma was taken up the handsome staircase which led to a wide passageway with another enormous window at the far end, making the space seem attractive. Everywhere had been freshly painted, but she supposed that as the house was modern, it had not yet had time to become faded and dingy.

'Mr Ashfield's apartment is here, madam. Yours is adjacent, and has a pleasant view from your sitting room over the garden at the rear of the property.'

Everything about this house was more than Emma could have hoped for; Sergeant Ross had done well to find it at such short notice. Her bedchamber had a communicating door to the master suite and she made sure this was locked. There was a substantial dressing room, a bathing room, and an alcove directly under a window where Annie could do her mending.

One of the maids who had accompanied the luggage curtsied. 'There is hot water if you would care to refresh yourself, ma'am, and all your garments are safely pressed and put away.'

'Thank you. I hope your accommodation is satisfactory.'

The girl nodded. 'Ever so, ma'am. I'm sharing with Molly, and we've a window looking out onto the street.'

Emma dismissed the girl and handed Annie her bonnet, gloves and reticule. After she had completed her ablutions she was ready to explore her new abode. 'Annie, I shall be dressing for dinner. Please find something suitable.'

The left-hand side of the corridor contained the master suite and her own rooms, but she had yet to investigate the doors on the right. These were presumably the guest bedchambers, all with dressing rooms and sitting rooms of their own. Emma followed the passageway and turned left to find another set of stairs which led to the nursery, school room and several other chambers. She discovered a third, much smaller staircase that must lead to the servants' rooms, but she had no intention of invading their privacy.

She made her way to the ground floor and was pleased to find no servant lurking there. The rectangular entrance hall had a bright and sunny study-cum-library to the left of the front door, and on the right was the drawing room. This was furnished in the Egyptian style, the furniture having gilt feet and a parade of peacocks marching over the upholstery.

Well satisfied with what she had found, Emma moved to one of the large windows that faced the street. The road outside was quiet; presumably the ladies of the houses were inside going about their business, and the gentlemen were away at their offices. She had no idea if morning calls were made in this stratum of society, but assumed that they were.

She found the bell-strap and pulled it sharply. A few minutes later there was a tap on the door and the butler appeared. 'I should like tea and cake, if any is available,' Emma told him. 'What time did Mr Ashfield say he would be returning to dine?'

'The master said dinner should be served at six o'clock, madam.'

Drinking tea and eating cake took up half an hour, and then Emma decided she would take a turn in the garden.

She was still wearing her travelling boots, and as the weather was clement there was no need for her to put on a pelisse. She certainly had no intention of wearing gloves or a bonnet to walk around her borrowed garden.

There was a smaller chamber leading from the drawing room in which there was a pianoforte and a harpsichord. French doors led from this onto a flagstone terrace that was enclosed by a stone balustrade. Eagerly, Emma unlatched the doors and stepped out into the warm summer sunshine. She remembered that during her last visit to London the air had been heavy with fumes, not at all like the fresh air of the countryside. However, this side of Town was less industrial, and the air was almost as fresh as at home. There were giant troughs of flowers on the flagstones, and the perfume from the pinks was strong enough to drown out the city fumes.

A flight of steps led to the garden and, picking up her skirt, Emma ran lightly down them. The garden was rectangular in shape. On the left were the outbuildings (presumably the stables, coach house and so on), and a red-brick wall continued down the length of the garden on the other side, making the space quite private. Of course, it would be possible to view the gardens on either side of the dividing wall from the upstairs windows, but not from the garden itself.

Whoever had designed this garden must obviously love flowers. There was a rose garden and herbaceous beds, as well as a substantial area of neatly clipped grass. Trees had been planted to give shade and shape, and the whole was quite delightful.

After spending an hour or so wandering about, Emma was ready to go inside. The church clock had struck the hour; she must go inside and change or she would be late for dinner. She was crossing the terrace when Sam emerged through the French doors. She had been about to address him by his real name but managed to stop the words escaping. 'Good afternoon, sir. I am glad to see you are back. I am more than pleased with this house; it has everything I asked for and more. However did you find such a property at such short notice?'

His eyes twinkled and he held out his arm for her to place her hand on it. 'I am pleased that you like it, my dear. We are fortunate indeed to have come across this house before anyone else. I have much to tell you. Do you wish to hear it now, or wait until we meet to dine?'

'I should like to hear it immediately. We could sit here in the music room where we will not be overheard.'

Sam guided her to another satin-covered sofa, brightly patterned with exotic birds. He waited until she was comfortably settled and then took the chair opposite. 'We forgot to discuss what business I'm actually involved in. I had thought that shipping would do; although we're a goodly distance from the docks, it's not inconceivable that a husband might wish his wife to reside somewhere more salubrious than the East End.'

'I shall play the part of a wife who knows nothing at all about her husband's business interests. Indeed, I knew little about Richard's business apart from that he had — or used to have — a fortune invested in various manufactories. It is this money that has been purloined.'

'Excellent — that will do very well. It would also explain my lengthy absences if I'm having to make my way to the other side of London. Now, Collins and I have been making discreet enquiries and have discovered the whereabouts of Mr Stanton.' He paused and his expression changed from friendly to formidable. 'Strangely enough, he has recently moved from rooms in Albemarle Street to a fancy address in Cavendish Square. He now has a carriage, several bang-up horses and a small army of flunkies at his beck and call.'

'He is living on the money he has stolen from me. If he has spent it already, there is little likelihood of my recovering what is missing.' Emma clenched her hands and bit her lip. 'I care not for the money, but I will have justice. I shall not rest until that man is ruined and in jail for his crimes.'

'Would you wish your family name to be dragged through the courts? Wouldn't you prefer him to be driven abroad to live in penury on the continent?'

'What I would really like is for him to meet the same end as my husband. That would be true justice.'

Sam stared at her for a moment as if assessing her resolve. 'I agree he deserves to die, but I'm not in the business of executions. I'll build a case against him, and then you must decide if you wish to press charges or banish him.'

The rage passed as quickly as it had come, and she was ashamed of her outburst. 'I beg your pardon, sir. Of course I do not wish you to kill him. What I should have said is that I would not be sorry if he died, but I would be content if he were ruined and sent abroad forever.'

'Stanton is to hold a soirée at the end

of next week; somehow we must obtain an invitation, as I need to search his house for evidence and have no wish to alert him by breaking in.'

Emma could not prevent her gasp of surprise. 'Break in? Good heavens, I did not know a runner was obliged to break the law in order to arrest the lawbreakers.'

Sam's smile brought colour to her cheeks. 'I do what I have to, my dear. Often the end justifies the means. Now, are we to change for dinner tonight?'

'We are, sir, and I must do so right away or I shall not be ready in time. I have met the butler and housekeeper and found them satisfactory. What of the rest of the staff?'

He was now on his feet and standing rather too close, making her feel a trifle insecure. 'There are a dozen of them, and they were all delighted to be kept on, as our landlord had told them they might well be dismissed.'

'Thank you for your hard work this afternoon, sir.'

'Enough of that *sir* nonsense. Either address me by my given name, or call me 'my dear' — I refuse to answer to *sir* any longer. We're supposed to be husband and wife, not strangers.'

Emma stepped away, almost treading on her skirt in her haste. 'My mother referred to my father as 'my lord', and he addressed her in similar fashion. I know not how they spoke in private, but I never heard them use anything else but their titles in public. Use your given name? I should think not. If you do not like to be referred to as 'sir', then I shall call you Mr Ashfield. You can have no objection to that, I'm sure.'

For a moment she thought he might argue the point, but instead he relaxed and half-smiled. 'Very well. I bow to your superior knowledge of how things are done by my betters.' Something flashed in his eyes and his lips twitched. 'However, I reserve the right to address you as I think fit. After all, I'm the master here, am I not?'

This ridiculous conversation had

gone on quite long enough. 'Do as you please. I know my views are of no account to you. We have yet to come up with a way to obtain invitations to this party, and I must give it some thought whilst I am changing.'

Sam watched her run away and thought he might have had the better of that exchange. He had no wish to take her to a party where she might be in danger, but he could think of no alternative. There was a strange warmth in his chest, something he was not accustomed to. Could this possibly be happiness?

She had loved the house and congratulated him on his part in renting it; and although it had been mere good fortune and had taken no skill or industry on his part, he'd enjoyed her praise. He knew nothing about grand ladies — had never been in love; but he was damn sure what he was beginning to feel for this exciting, intelligent, lovely young woman would only lead to heartache for both of them if he did not knock it on the head immediately.

7

Emma took far longer over her preparations than she was accustomed to. She wanted to look her best tonight, as this was the first meal she had eaten in her new persona of Mrs Ashfield. Whilst she sat on her dressing stool having her hair arranged, she closed her eyes and turned her thoughts to the tricky problem of obtaining an invitation to that villain's soirée.

The obvious solution was to somehow meet Stanton and get him to extend an invitation himself. Although this would be far simpler if the man were married, she was relieved that he was not, for that would mean causing distress to an innocent bystander.

'There, ma'am. You look a picture, if you don't mind my saying so. Although we only brought with us your plainest gowns, the forget-me-not blue cambric matches your eyes exactly.'

'Thank you, Annie. You have done well. If I'm honest, I prefer a simple ensemble — all the frills and furbelows that are fashionable nowadays are not to my liking.' She stood up and shook out the skirt of her gown in case it had become creased after having been sat on for so long. 'I shall not be late tonight, Annie. I have no wish to spend the evening with . . . with my husband.' She had been about to say 'Sergeant Ross', but realised there was an unknown chambermaid moving about next door.

The novelty of living in a smaller and more convenient home had yet to wear off, and Emma almost skipped her way along the corridor and down the staircase. But then she hesitated, not sure if she should go straight to the dining room, or into the drawing room for a pre-dinner drink as she had used to do with Richard.

The butler glided up to her and bowed. 'Madam, the master is on the terrace and would like you to join him there for a glass of champagne.'

Emma nodded and walked briskly to the French doors, wondering how their limited budget had run to such an expensive beverage. The sergeant — for he would remain that in the privacy of her own thoughts — was staring out into the garden, and a footman lurked with a tray upon which were two glasses of the sparkling drink.

'Good evening. What exactly are we celebrating?' She had not meant her comment to sound so snippy, but it was too late to retract it. He spun as if stabbed by a hatpin and scowled at her.

'We are celebrating, my dear, our arrival in London and drinking to the success of our business venture.'

She took a glass from the tray and the footman vanished, no doubt relieved to leave them to their bickering. She sipped the wine without comment, trying to organise her words and ask a question without offending him again. 'I thought we were on a restricted budget, sir. I did not expect to be drinking such a thing as champagne.'

His expression changed and he grinned, making him look years younger and far less grim. 'And neither did I, my dear. But the owners of this property have left their wine cellar for our use.' He swallowed his drink in two gulps. 'I've not had cat-lap before. Not sure I'll bother to have it again; it's a lady's drink in my opinion. I prefer beer — I know where I am with that.'

'Beer? I suppose that's what a common soldier would drink, but you are a gentleman now and must force yourself to drink wines, spirits, and the occasional glass of champagne.'

He put the glass down with such force the slender stem snapped and he swore. 'Dammit to hell! I expect breakages will have to be paid for.' He seemed more outraged at this thought than the fact that there was blood dripping from a deep cut on his palm.

Without conscious thought, Emma hurried across to him. 'Hold your hand up; it will stem the bleeding. Do you have a handkerchief we can tie around it until I can find a proper bandage? I fear you will require the attentions of a physician.'

He looked at his hand in surprise. 'I didn't realise I'd cut myself. It's not as bad as it looks. I've no need for a quack.' He delved into his jacket and produced a clean white handkerchief.

Emma flicked it from his fingers and carefully tied it around his palm. 'There, that will do for now. However, I think you had better get your valet to attend to it before we dine. I have no wish to watch blood dripping into your dinner.'

Sam chuckled, something she had not heard him do before, and for some reason her pulse skipped a beat. 'I shall do as you ask, my dear. As you know, I'm the most biddable and meek of husbands.' He winked at her and then strolled off into the house. She noticed he kept his injured hand elevated, so it would seem he did not completely ignore her instructions.

Less than quarter of an hour later, he reappeared and dinner was announced. He was about to step aside and allow Emma to precede him, when she smiled. 'It will be expected that we walk in together. I do not have precedence here; I am your wife, and therefore of less importance.' Obediently he held out his arm and she rested her hand on it, unsurprised by the strength she detected beneath the fabric of his jacket sleeve.

Fortunately they had been placed on either side of the large table, instead of at either end, and were thus able to converse without shouting. They discussed nothing much at all until the dessert had been served and the flunkies sent about their business. Then Emma told Sam what she had come up with.

'The only way we are going to get an invitation to this party is if we manage to meet Stanton somewhere, or inveigle an introduction to friends of his that are already going. Is it possible you can discover some of the names of the guests on the list? There must be other couples; perhaps I can call in on one of the wives and mention the fact that we are recently in Town and know nobody.'

'I reckon Collins might be able to do that. He has struck up a friendship with the kitchen maid at Stanton's new home.'

Emma shook her head sadly. 'I fear that will be of little use to us, as a kitchen maid will have no knowledge of what goes on above stairs. He would do better to cultivate the under-footman — they always know everything that is going on in an establishment.'

'Is that so?' He looked remarkably smug for a gentleman who had just been told his plan was flawed. 'What about if the kitchen maid is walking out with the under-footman? Do you think that might work?'

'I suppose that would serve the purpose. However, I am not comfortable with your man playing fast and loose with the affections of a young girl in order to obtain information. Surely the offer of money would be enough?'

He reached out for the decanter of sweet wine that had been served to drink with the marchpane and blancmange, but then hesitated and his hand dropped back. This reminded Emma of his earlier injury, and she was concerned to see the bandage was no longer white, but red where it ran across his palm. 'You need sutures in that cut, Mr Ashfield. If you will not have the doctor, then I must do it for you. I'm sure it can be no harder than stitching a hole in a sheet.'

'Good idea. I've done the same for my comrades on the battlefield many a time. I've got the necessary items in my rooms, so we might as well do it there.'

She had expected him to refuse and had been ready to insist the physician be sent for, and was not sure if she was prepared to actually push the needle through his skin herself. Now she had no option but to do as she had offered. If he was happy to suffer at her hands, then who was she to cavil?

Sam was on his feet and out through the dining room door before she could protest about his suggestion that she stitch him up in his apartment. His lips twitched: he doubted a lady of quality would have the courage to do it, but was eager to see at what point she gave up. He was about to stride down to the kitchens himself to fetch a kettle of boiling water and some basins and clean cloth for bandages, when he recalled in time that he was no longer a member of the lower orders, but a gentleman who must ring for attention. He spotted a lurking footman and told him what he needed and where to bring it.

Lady Emma ran lightly up the stairs, exposing a delightful amount of trim ankle in the process. No doubt she was going to fetch her sewing basket, and would join him in his dressing room when she had what she needed.

'My dear,' he yelled up the stairs, causing her to miss her step, 'you'll need to use a fine needle and silk thread.'

She regained her balance and turned to glare at him. 'Kindly refrain from shouting, Mr Ashfield. I am not hard of hearing.'

Unrepentant, he bounded up behind her. 'I never thought you were, my love. And as I'm master in my home, I'll do as I please.' Her cheeks coloured at his comment and he couldn't hold back his laughter. 'Come along, let's get this done before I drip my gore all over the smart carpet.'

He'd dismissed his valet, telling him he was quite capable of putting himself to bed, but somehow word had spread about his injury and his man was in the sitting room. There was already a jug of steaming water, a basin and several neatly rolled bandages waiting to be used.

Sam nodded his thanks and continued to his bedchamber, where he rummaged through his bags until he found the parcel he needed. As he was removing it he tried to think of the last time he had used the needle, thread and scissors. It had to be three years ago at least. He grimaced. Perhaps it would be better to use whatever Lady Emma supplied.

He replaced the package and tossed the saddlebags back into the closet. She was there already, and busy at the table, sorting through her sewing box. He was pleased to see there was a bottle of brandy on there too. He was going to need a swig or two before this was done. With a sigh of resignation, he picked up a straight-backed wooden chair and hefted it across the carpet, then sat. He quickly unwound the sodden bandage and put his hand palm uppermost on the clean cloth that had been spread over the top of the wooden surface.

'God's teeth!' he exclaimed. 'It's worse than I thought. It's going to need half a dozen stitches. Are you up to that task?' He looked at her and could see no sign of queasiness or fear.

'Allow me, ma'am — I am somewhat of an expert in this field,' Benton said, picking up the brandy and tipped a quantity of it over the gash.

'Buggeration! That's for drinking, not wasting, man.' Sam snatched the bottle and gulped several mouthfuls down. The warmth of the spirit as it hit his throat steadied his nerves. He was relieved Lady Emma wasn't going to sew him up. Having his hand touched by her would be torment.

'If you would care to hold steady, sir, I shall begin.' His valet stepped in so that his body was shielding the table as if he thought Sam might faint away if he watched a needle being pushed through his flesh.

'Get on with it, man. I'm bleeding all over the carpet.' He closed his eyes and gritted his teeth, waiting for the first stab of the needle. Then something extraordinary occurred which quite took his mind off what Benton was doing. Lady Emma moved to his side and took his free hand in hers.

'I was quite prepared to do the sutures myself, but your valet would probably do a quicker and more efficient job,' she said. 'I shall hold your hand until he has finished.'

She was so close to him that he could smell her perfume; he was sure it was bergamot and roses. The hand was small and soft within his own, and when the needle went in he pretended to be in pain and closed his fingers around hers. This was a different sort of agony, but he would endure a hundred stitches if it meant he could hold her hand again.

His hand was repaired far too quickly and he had no option but to release his grip. 'Thank you, Benton. I'm obliged to you.' The valet stepped aside so Sam could view his handiwork. 'Excellent job; I couldn't have done it better myself. I doubt I'll even have a scar.' He had hoped Emma (she would be without her title when he thought of her from now on) might bandage his wound, but she patted his shoulder and moved away.

'I doubt you will be able to hold the

reins of your horse tomorrow, Mr Ashfield, so perhaps I could prevail upon you to accompany me in the carriage when I go out.'

The way he felt at the moment, he thought this was a bad idea, but he could hardly tell her why he didn't want to spend time alone with her. 'Of course, my love. I'd be delighted to see the sights with you. Did you have any particular destination in mind?'

'Not at the moment, but I intend to ask the housekeeper where I should go first. I cannot tell you how thrilled I am to be in London. It was kind of you to bring me on your business trip.'

His hand was now encased in a fresh white bandage and he was free to stand up. 'I'm at your command, my dear, and you may tell me where we're going when we meet at breakfast tomorrow morning.'

Before she could move away, he stepped in closer and kissed her lightly on the cheek. Her mouth rounded in shock and he winked. She could hardly protest, as Benton was still in the room with them.

'Good night, my dear. I've letters to read and must return to the study.' He stepped around her and strolled down the passageway, feeling that tonight had been a resounding success. After seeing Emma's wifely devotion and his affectionate kiss, no one could doubt that they were indeed a happily married couple.

He had almost reached the study when he understood the enormity of his error. Dammit to hell! There had been no need for artifice with Benton; he knew very well how things were.

* * *

Emma watched him saunter away and wished she had a book to throw at him. He was deliberately provoking her and she did not enjoy the experience one bit. She took a steadying breath and smiled at Benton. 'We are grateful for your help. I had quite forgotten you were skilled in medical matters. I bid you good night.'

'Forgive me for speaking out of turn, madam, but would you like me to speak to Mrs Philips tonight on your behalf? I'm sure she will then be able to come up with several suggestions and have them ready for you tomorrow.'

'That would be an excellent notion. Mr Ashfield is going to be very busy, and I would dearly like to make the acquaintance of other ladies in a similar position. Perhaps Phillips might know the names of my neighbours so I could leave a card.'

'I am sure I will have what you require by breakfast time.' He bowed and she nodded.

Annie was waiting for her and was agog for news of the accident. 'Imagine being able to sit without flinching whilst someone sews you up. I didn't know that Benton was able to do such a thing.'

'Neither did I, but then I rarely saw him before this. He intends to ask the housekeeper for a list of the names of our neighbours. I was thinking I would leave a card, but I do not have any printed so will have to write them out myself. You can go now; I shall occupy myself with this task until I retire.'

By the time she had written a dozen cards, Emma was almost beginning to believe she really was Mrs Ashfield. She had never had the opportunity to do any play-acting before — 'children out of sight' was the rule of the house in which she had grown up — and was rather enjoying the experience.

Only as she was drifting off to sleep did she realise that there had been no need to dissemble in front of Benton. Her hand-holding and the sergeant's kiss had been quite unnecessary. What had possessed both of them to carry the masquerade so far?

8

The list supplied by the housekeeper was comprehensive and exactly what Emma wanted, and she handed it to Sam once they were in the study. 'I have written a dozen cards. All I need to do is address them, and then one of the footmen can take some later this morning. Whilst he is delivering them, he can enquire if the lady of the house will be receiving callers this afternoon.'

Sam perused the list with disinterest until he came across a name that he recognised. 'This is better than I'd hoped — Mr and Mrs Forsyth are also on the guest list for the party.'

This was news indeed. 'I had no idea you had discovered anyone's name on that list. How did you achieve this?'

'Collins was successful and obtained the names of half a dozen guests. I cannot believe our luck that two happen to be residing in our neighbourhood.'

'How can you know that the Mr and Mrs Forsyth on your list are the same Mr and Mrs Forsyth on mine?'

He shrugged and settled more comfortably in the armchair opposite. 'I don't, but we'll visit and discover for ourselves if they are indeed friends of Stanton's.'

'It might not be as simple as that, Mr Ashfield. We cannot call until we receive a card in return, and that might not happen.'

He leaned forward and frowned. 'I'll be damned if I'll be referred to by my wife as 'Mr Ashfield'. If you will not use my given name, then use nothing at all.'

He was taking this play-acting a mite too seriously, Emma thought, but she had no time to reprimand him as there was a polite tap on the door and the butler came in. 'Mrs Ashfield, I have sent the footmen with your cards. Do you wish to be informed immediately if there is any response? I have warned

Mrs Philips that there could be morning callers this afternoon.'

'Thank you, Foster. That is very efficient of you. As you know, Mr Ashfield and I are going out soon; you can give me any cards on my return.' The butler bowed and retreated.

Sam was having difficulty controlling his amusement. 'Good God! What nonsense is this? How can you have morning callers in the afternoon?'

'I know it is quite ridiculous, but morning calls take place between two o'clock and five o'clock. I can only suppose this is because members of the *ton* do not rise until midday, and therefore their day doesn't start until then.'

He shook his head in disbelief. 'The more I learn about my betters, the less I understand. A regular person gets up at dawn and goes to bed when it's dark — but I suppose the swells don't need to work for a living, so can please themselves when they rise.'

The rattle of a carriage coming up

outside interrupted their conversation. 'The carriage is here. I must run upstairs and put on my bonnet and gloves and collect my reticule. I shall not be a moment.'

The front door was open when Emma returned, and Sam was standing on the front step gazing down the road. She joined him, and when he held out his arm she slipped her hand through it without protest. If she did not know the truth, she would think he was a gentleman born. He handed her into the carriage and settled opposite her on the squabs. The door slammed and the coachman flicked his whip.

They had been travelling for a while when he broke the silence. 'I reckon it's a mile or two to Bond Street. On horseback we'd be there in no time. Getting through the streets in a carriage is tedious.'

'I have my jewellery with me. I think it would be sensible for you to sell it. They are family pieces — old-fashioned, but they have no sentimental value for me. I am quite certain you do not wish to accompany me to the various emporiums I intend to visit, so I thought you could undertake that task whilst I am browsing.' She opened her reticule and removed the velvet bag, which she tossed across to him.

'I'm reluctant to do this,' he said, 'but you have the right of it. Most of my blunt went on the advance rental for the house, and if we wish to remain solvent whilst we solve this business we're going to need funds.'

'I'm sure you will know the best place to get a good price. I have asked the coachman to drop me first. I thought we could meet at Gunter's in Berkeley Square. I can walk there easily from Bond Street, and the carriage will have no difficulty finding a space to wait.'

'I'm not sure that's a good idea. It's the haunt of the toffs and someone might recognise you. I don't think we should risk it.'

'I spent just one season in Town, and

that was more than five years ago. I think it extremely unlikely there will be anyone in the city in midsummer who might remember me. I am determined to have an ice and will not be deterred.' She waited for him to argue, but he half-smiled and raised his hands as if in defeat, then pulled out a battered silver pocket watch.

'It's now a little after eleven o'clock. At what time do you intend to be there? And another thing — why did you not bring your maid with you? I'm not happy with the idea of you wandering about unescorted.'

Emma smiled. 'In my old persona you would be correct. But remember I'm the wife of a successful business-man, not a member of the aristocracy, and therefore I have the freedom to move about the place on my own. Shall we say one o'clock?'

They arrived in Bond Street eventu-ally, and a groom scrambled down to open the carriage door. Emma emerged into the sunlight and looked around in delight. For the first time in her life she could do as she pleased, wandering in and out of shops and passing unnoticed in the crowd. Being a commoner was turning out to be more interesting than she had expected.

Sam had got out with her and had a quick conversation with the coachman before turning back to her. 'Take care of yourself, my dear. I should not wish anything untoward to happen to you.'

He was about to step away when, to her horror, she saw a well-dressed gentleman approaching who would recognise her. He had been a friend of her husband's and had visited Whitford Hall once.

'What is it? Have you seen someone you know?'

She nodded. Before she could protest, Sam pulled her into an embrace and tilted her bonnet towards him so her features were obscured. His quick reaction prevented a disaster, and the man strolled past, unaware of Emma's identity.

Her chest was hard against his; she could feel his heat through the flimsy muslin of her gown. Something strange flickered through her — something she did not recognise; but then she was released and the moment passed. She was almost certain she'd heard the man, Mr Palmer, tutting as he walked past. Sam's smile was infectious and she could not help but return it.

'That was close, but most enjoyable,' Sam said. 'I just hope that cove was the only one in Bond Street who might recognise you.' He raised his hand and solemnly straightened Emma's bonnet, which had slipped sideways during their embrace. 'Mind you, wearing that monstrosity on your head makes you all but invisible. What in God's name possessed you to buy something that resembles a coal scuttle?'

'It's ridiculous, I know, which is why I have never worn it before today. It is also a trifle dated, which is ideal for our purposes, for the wife of a tradesman would not be in the forefront of fashion.' She stepped away, and he laughed and jumped back into the carriage.

The pavement was busy with like-minded pedestrians, and Emma began to feel uncomfortable without an escort. It wasn't because she was the only woman on her own, but because she was unsure of the direction in which to travel and did not like to ask in case she were recognised. The unexpected encounter with an acquaintance of Richard's had unsettled her, and she was beginning to regret her decision to parade in Bond Street, even though it was midsummer and all the important families would have removed themselves to their country estates. She had forgotten that Richard had not been an aristocrat, but primarily a businessman, and therefore his cronies might well be wandering around London even in the summer.

She stepped into a milliner's and spent a pleasant hour admiring bonnets and ribbons, coming away with a hatbox

that contained a pretty chip-straw con-
fection that she much preferred to the
one she was wearing at present. After
meandering along the streets, she decided
she would make her way to Berkeley
Square in the hope that the time was
nearing one o'clock — she had heard a
nearby church strike midday a considerable time ago. There appeared to be a
steady stream of ladies with parasols
heading in the same direction; no doubt
the warm weather made everyone's thoughts
turn to a cooling ice.

Berkeley Square was a pleasant place
to be on a hot day. The lime trees gave
welcome shade, and Emma was delighted
to see her carriage stationary amongst
several others. She was about to hurry
over when she saw Sam lounging against
the carriage door, talking to a smartly
dressed stranger. He saw her approaching and straightened. His smile made
her believe for an instant that she was
really his wife and a woman that he
cared for.

'My dear, you're early — not

something I expected of you. Allow me to introduce a new acquaintance of mine. Mr Waters, this is my wife.' Emma nodded and he did the same.

'I'm delighted to meet you, Mrs Ashfield. Mr Ashfield has been kind enough to invite my wife and me to dine with you tonight. We too are in London temporarily, and my dear wife is becoming lonely away from her family and friends.'

'I shall look forward to seeing you both tonight. My dear, do we have time for an ice before we return home?'

Sam nodded. 'If you would care to sit in the carriage, my love, I'll fetch you one immediately. I bid you good day, sir, and look forward to seeing you this evening.'

His new friend raised a hand in casual salute and walked away. Emma wanted to know who he was, and how Sam had met him; but her pretend-husband headed towards Gunter's leaving the under-coachman to assist her into the carriage.

Fortunately both doors had been left open and the interior of the vehicle was pleasantly cool. She had noticed as she crossed the square that each carriage was similarly occupied. Her head was unpleasantly hot and she wished to remove her hideous bonnet, but hesitated. Had she better wait until they were away from this busy square before she made herself more recognisable?

She untied the ribbons and decided she would take the risk. As soon as the bonnet was sitting on the squabs beside her, she felt much cooler. A few minutes later, the carriage rocked and Sam appeared, carrying a dish of ice cream.

'Here you are. You must eat it quickly, as it's already melting.'

Emma took a spoonful. 'It's quite delicious. Are you not having any yourself?'

'I've already had one, and very tasty it was too. You'll be pleased to hear that my business this morning has been completed satisfactorily. I met Mr

Waters on a similar errand and we got talking. Perhaps I shouldn't have asked them to dine without speaking to you first. I'm not versed in the etiquette of married couples.'

Between spoonfuls, Emma replied: 'You are master of the house and make these decisions. It is for the wife to accommodate her husband's wishes as best she can.'

'That is as likely to happen as are pigs to fly, my dear. I doubt you've a biddable bone in your body.' He leaned across and removed the empty dish and spoon from her fingers. When he held it outside the door, it vanished; no doubt the under-groom was running back to the shop with it.

Once the carriage was in motion, Emma felt it safe to ask about her jewellery. When Sam told her the astounding amount he had obtained, she was all but speechless. 'Good heavens! We are wealthy indeed. I should like you to hire me a hack so that I might ride out with you each morning. I know the park is some distance away, but not so far we cannot go there. I think it unlikely I will be seen by anyone who knows me if we remain on this side of Town.'

'I'll ask Collins to do that, and look forward to accompanying you as soon as I've acquired a suitable nag.' He pointed to her discarded bonnet. 'I hope you're never going to wear that monstrosity again. It doesn't suit you.'

When had he become an arbitrator of fashion? 'I have purchased another; no doubt you have seen the hatbox on the seat beside me. I can't remember the last time I bought a new bonnet — as I rarely went out, and we did not mix with our neighbours, there was little point in refurbishing my wardrobe.'

'Being an ordinary fellow is so much simpler than being a gentleman. All this changing of clothes and tying of neckcloths isn't to my taste. Now, do you not want to know why I invited two perfect strangers to dine with us tonight?'

'I thought you had already told me. You said that Mr Waters was selling his wife's jewellery as you were.'

'Indeed I did, my love, but that was hardly sufficient for me to curry an acquaintance. It was when I heard him give his address that I knew he would be a valuable asset. They're lodging in Albemarle Street, and have been doing so for the past six weeks — it's possible that they'll have valuable information about our quarry.'

'In which case, I must applaud your decision to invite them to our home. I think we must not make the occasion too formal, as I have no wish to make either of them uncomfortable.'

'I'm hoping he might give us some indication as to where I might scrape an acquaintance with Stanton. Nothing remains private when you're living in lodgings, and it's quite possible Mr Waters will prove an invaluable acquaintance.'

The carriage settled into a companionable silence, and Emma did not feel the need to break it. How could she be so relaxed in this man's company when she had only known him so short a time? She was an unnatural woman to be gallivanting around the place, buying new bonnets and happily entertaining, when her real husband had only died a few days ago.

Then something extraordinary occurred to her. She sat up in her seat so suddenly that the hatbox shot across the carriage and landed in Sam's lap. Who was the more startled by this event, she could not tell. 'I do beg your pardon, but I just understood the truth about the past five years.'

Instead of laughing, his expression was serious, and he leaned forward in anticipation of her revelation.

'You will be shocked by what I'm going to tell you, but I cannot keep this to myself.' She couldn't meet his eyes whilst she spoke; she was too ashamed of what she was going to say. 'I find that I am relieved that my husband is dead. Our marriage was a sham from start to finish. He had no interest in me as a wife — I was merely window dressing.' She had been about to reveal that he had visited her bedchamber no more than three times in the five years they had been together, and that only in the first week of their union, but then reconsidered. Was the fact that he had spent more time alone with his male friends than he ever had with her of any significance?

'Go on,' Sam prompted her. 'What were you about to tell me?'

Emma's skin prickled and her palms were damp inside her cotton gloves. She wished heartily she had not started this inappropriate conversation. 'I have no wish to discuss such things with you; I should not have said anything.'

He nodded and sat back. 'That explains why you have no children. I did wonder. Of course you're relieved that you're now free to marry again and live a normal life. Your husband gave you sanctuary when you needed it and you ran his house for him. Now you can move on.' The coach rocked as he moved across to sit next to her. 'In the circumstances, sweetheart, do you still wish to continue with this escapade? Would you not prefer to put it all behind you and enjoy your independence?'

He was sitting too close; his thigh was all but touching hers. 'No, I cannot move on until justice has been done. Although I am glad to be released from a sterile union, I would not have had my husband murdered so cruelly in order to obtain my freedom. He did not deserve to die at the instigation of his half-brother.'

He took her hands in his and held them gently. 'In which case, we'll continue with the investigation. Do you think you could bring yourself to use my given name? I know we haven't been acquainted long, and I'm not of your social class, but I believe we've become friends nevertheless.'

Emma's heart was thumping as if it wished to escape from the confines of her bodice, and a strange, unfamiliar flickering heat had settled in a most unusual place. 'I have never used a gentleman's given name. It was not done in our household, as I explained to you. But I think it will be acceptable in these extraordinary circumstances to do as you ask. In future I shall address you as Samuel, and you may call me Emma.'

His fingers tightened for a second, and then he released his hold and he was back on the other side of the carriage. 'I should much prefer to be called Sam, but we'll settle for Samuel if that's as far as you're prepared to go.'

When they arrived at Tavistock Place, he did not wait for the coachman to descend and open the door, but did this himself and then kicked down the steps. He stepped out and turned to hand Emma down as if he had been doing this every day of his life. She was not the only one revelling in this masquerade.

'I should like to talk to you,' Emma

said. 'Shall we stroll around the garden for a while?'

'I would like that. We can go in through the stable yard.'

The stables were as well-kept as the house, and Emma was able to walk through without miring her skirts. There was a smart green-painted door in the wall at the far end of the yard, and Sam escorted her to it. 'This takes us into the garden,' she said. 'I noticed it yesterday.'

Once they were private again, she led him to the stone bench she had discovered in the rose arbour. 'I know nothing about you,' she began. 'Will you please tell me how you came to be a senior investigator at Bow Street?'

9

Sam had guessed this moment would come and had prepared an edited version of his past life, but for some reason he wished to tell her the unvarnished truth. 'The only good thing about my birth is that I am not a bastard; my parents were wed. My pa was head groom at a grand house in Hertfordshire, and my ma was the cook until they married. I have two sisters. I had two brothers, but they both died in infancy.'

'How sad. Did you join your father as a groom?'

'I did, but something happened and I was forced to leave in a hurry.' He glanced at her but she wasn't looking shocked, merely curious. 'The owner of the property — a titled gentleman — had two sons, and the youngest was a nasty bit of work. I found him raping my sister and I killed him.'

He had expected Emma to leap to her feet, to run away, but instead she did something quite extraordinary. She stretched out and took his hand. 'How dreadful. I am not surprised you did what you did. Any brother would have done the same. Are you still a wanted man? Is that why you haven't told me the name of your employer?'

'I am. My name is not Ross. It's better if I don't tell you what it is. I've been living in the expectation that I will be denounced as a murderer at any time. My parents gave me what money they had — which was precious little, and I fled. Fortunately for me, there was a recruiting drive going through the next town, and I took the King's shilling. I fought against the Frenchies and left with a small amount in the funds from my prize money, and joined the runners. The life suits me, as I have no ties.'

'That must have been many years ago. Surely the family will no longer be searching for you. Do you think your father lost his position? Have you ever tried to contact them?'

'I haven't, and there's not a single day goes past that I don't think about it. But I can't risk it.'

If Emma didn't remove her hand from his, he was going to do something he would regret. He'd just told her he was living a lie and was a murderer on the run. Why was she still holding his hand?

'Then I shall make enquiries for you,' she said. 'Come to think of it, as Mr and Mrs Ashfield we can do so together. When we have finished here we will continue this pretence and take a trip to Hertfordshire. I'm certain no one will associate a runaway groom with a prosperous businessman with a completely different name and a smart wife on his arm.'

Her smile did something strange to Sam's insides, and he couldn't prevent the voluntary tightening of his grip. Then her expression changed, and he forced his fingers to relax so she could remove her hands from his.

'When were you thinking of going on this excursion?' he asked her. 'Before or after you send your brother-in-law to the gallows?'

'Once we have obtained an invitation to the party next week, we can go to Hertfordshire. I believe that county is not too far from London. Could we get there and back in a day?'

'If we travelled post we could, but the horses couldn't take a double journey without a rest overnight.' The thought of spending a night at an inn in Emma's company was almost too much for Sam's control. 'However, although we are well-breeched at present, I don't think it's sensible to waste money on posting when we can drive. The price of an overnight stay would be a fraction of the posting costs.'

'In which case we must find somewhere pleasant to stay the night. I suppose we should take your valet and my maid if we wish to appear well-to-do.'

'I have no wish to share the carriage with either of them,' Sam said firmly. 'Can't you manage without someone to dress you just for one night?'

Instead of flying into the boughs at his comment, Emma laughed. 'I may be high in the instep, but I am perfectly capable of taking care of myself if need be. More to the point, sir, will you be able to maintain the facade of a gentleman for so long without blaspheming or cursing?'

This conversation had continued long enough, Sam decided — they were becoming intimate, and it wasn't a good idea. In a few weeks he must return to his low existence and she to her stately home. He would do nothing to jeopardise her good name, however much he might wish to. 'We had better go in, my love. You have yet to inform the housekeeper we're having dinner guests this evening. Also, it's possible we might have a pile of cards to view in response to the ones you sent out this morning to our neighbours.'

He stood up and offered his hand to help her to her feet, but she shook her head and rose gracefully. Then she fussed with her skirts, which looked perfectly fine to him, and waited, tapping her foot, so he was obliged to put his arm out for her to use.

He decided that tonight he would play the loving husband in front of their guests, as she would be unable to reprimand him without revealing their deception. He glanced down at her glorious golden hair and wondered what it would be like to run his fingers through it. But he pushed the thought away — frustration and madness lay in that direction.

* * *

Sergeant Ross — no, he must be Samuel to her now — escorted her into the house and then strode off, muttering something about urgent business in the study. Foster handed her a silver salver, upon which was a satisfactory

150

pile of cards. When she asked him to inform Cook and the housekeeper of their evening plans, he nodded.

'It is going to be a warm evening, madam. Would you care to dine on the terrace?'

'Eat outside? I have never done so in the evening, but I think the idea quite delightful.'

She took the cards to the far end of the drawing room and found herself a comfortable seat out of the sunlight, in a position where the cool breeze from the garden reached her. The footman had delivered a dozen cards and all but one of the recipients had responded. Three of the cards said they would be receiving visitors that afternoon, four contained no more than a short welcome to the area, and the others said they would be calling in to introduce themselves today. If Emma were to change before the first of these people arrived, she had better return to her rooms immediately. Unfortunately, the missing response was from Mrs Forsyth.

In the vestibule she waylaid a footman and told him there would be morning callers, that tea and biscuits would be required, and that both parlourmaids would be needed to serve. Then, finding the study door ajar, she knocked softly and pushed it open. Samuel was pacing the carpet, his expression one she had not seen before. Surely he could not be flustered at the thought of standing host at his first dinner party?

'I'm sorry to intrude, but I have come to warn you we will be having a succession of visitors this very afternoon,' Emma told him. 'I doubt that any gentlemen will come, but it might be as well for you to put in a brief appearance just in case there's someone you can discreetly question.'

'What about Mrs Forsyth?'

She shook her head and explained there had been no response from them.

'Dammit! I'll find the man who took the card and see if I can discover any more about the family. If they're cronies of Stanton, then they might not be pleasant people.'

'I think it unlikely that Mrs Forsyth will be involved in anything nefarious. Hopefully she will send around her card later today.'

Sam tugged at his cravat, which became unravelled, giving him a rakish air. 'Do I have to change my raiment, or will I do as I am?'

'I was about to say that you would pass muster, but now you will have to return to your rooms and get your valet to replace your neckcloth. I shall change my gown — it's what ladies do in the afternoon.'

'We agreed we would not change for dinner, did we not?'

'I fear you have a lot to learn about the habits of a gentlewoman. We have morning gowns; promenade gowns; gowns for driving, dancing and taking tea. Oh, let's not forget about evening gowns and ball gowns.'

'You cannot be serious — no sane person could possibly require so many outfits in the day.'

'It is required of one, if one moves in the *ton*.' His expression was one of bewilderment and she took pity on him. 'Even when I had my season five years ago, I never changed my ensemble less than four times. It is so much easier for a gentleman — they have riding clothes, everyday garments and evening clothes. Ladies are not expected to do much more than look decorative and run the house — which is why, I am sure, many of them spend so much time on their wardrobes.'

She turned to go, but as she did so someone knocked on the front door. Not wishing to be seen lurking in the corridor, she stepped back into the study, but remained by the open door so she could overhear what was said. There was no exchange of words and the front door closed.

Foster hurried towards her with a note in his hand; he had forgotten to put it on the salver. 'This was delivered for you, madam.'

Emma took the proffered paper and broke the seal.

Dear Mrs Ashfield
  I apologise for not responding sooner to your card, but I am presently indisposed. I am not receiving visitors at the moment.
  Yours sincerely
  Mrs Forsyth

'Well, that explains why we didn't hear before this. If Mrs Forsyth is unwell, perhaps I might call in a day or two and see if I can offer any assistance.'

Instead of pulling the bell-strap, Sam stepped out into the corridor and yelled for the butler to come at once. It was certainly quicker to do this, but was not the action of a gentleman. He had a disturbing tendency to shout, but no doubt she would become accustomed to it in time.

Foster could be heard thundering towards them and, despite her disapproval, Emma could not prevent her smile. 'Your unorthodox method has certainly produced the desired results, Samuel.'

He grinned and threw open the door just as the butler arrived. 'Come in, man. I have questions for you. What do you know about Mr and Mrs Forsyth, who reside over the road?'

'I thought I recognised the messenger, sir. Mr Forsyth is a businessman and is away a lot of the time. Mrs Forsyth is said to be an invalid.' He offered no further information, but Sam was not satisfied with this answer.

'You're not telling me the whole. Out with it, if you please.'

'What I am about to tell you, Mr Ashfield, I cannot substantiate. It is merely hearsay. Mr Forsyth is said to be a man of violent temper, and his staff rarely stay longer than a week or two. They have not been in the neighbourhood more than a few months.'

When the butler retreated, Emma turned to Samuel: 'From his tone, one would think Mr and Mrs Forsyth were not welcome around here. Your man Collins must make enquiries downstairs, for I'm sure there is more to know about that family.'

'It's a damn shame you cannot visit today. We might have been able to attend a party on their coat-tails.'

'Never mind,' Emma said with a sigh. 'I have great hopes we will do better with Mr and Mrs Waters when they come this evening.'

'That's a capital idea. What time are we expecting the influx of visitors? I intend to make myself scarce unless you send for me. I'd rather have my teeth pulled than drink a dish of tea with a lot of simpering young ladies and their doting mamas.'

★   ★   ★

After a succession of callers, none of whom brought a gentleman with them, Emma was relieved to have the drawing room to herself again. She had discovered nothing of any import, apart from the pertinent fact that not one of the ladies had visited Mrs Forsyth. They had all received the same reply to their initial overture. Either Mrs Forsyth was a permanent invalid, or she didn't wish to meet the ladies of the neighbourhood.

Fortunately, the visitors had come early in the afternoon, so Emma could now make some calls herself. No one had brought a maid with them, and they had all come on foot, so she thought she would do the same. However, before she left she would update Samuel on what little she had discovered.

He was lurking in the study, pretending to read the newspaper. 'Have they gone? Is it safe for me to emerge?'

'They were all perfectly pleasant ladies, Samuel, but none of them had anything of interest to tell us. Do you not think it strange Mrs Forsyth has yet to receive any visitors? If she had not been seen about the place, one would think she might not exist.'

He tossed the journal to one side. 'I

think this rather confirms my suspicions. If Forsyth is involved with Stanton, then he would not want the local busybodies in and out of his house. The fact that he has such a high turnover of servants is also suspicious.'

'Why is it suspicious? Surely if they are difficult to work for, then staff would leave of their own accord.'

'That's perfectly possible, but it could also be that Forsyth has no wish for anyone to be there long enough to discover his personal business. I already have Collins sniffing about. If there's anything to discover, my man will know by the end of the day.'

'I am now going to call on the four ladies who said they would be receiving this afternoon. Why don't you come with me?'

Sam laughed disparagingly. 'God forbid! I've discovered something in one of the papers we brought with us from Whitford Hall. Your husband also dealt with a company in the City, and I intend to visit them this afternoon.

You'll recall that there was a letter from London that day, but it had been taken by the murderer. It has to be significant.'

'Do you still think that Richard's murder was unintentional? That my brother-in-law sent a henchman to recover the letter, and on finding my husband in the study, killed him by accident?'

'I think that it was possible your husband recognised the man, which made his death inevitable. I'm sure Stanton wished the theft to remain undiscovered, and he'll be aware that this information will now have come to light. He must be concerned that he has heard nothing about the death. With hindsight, I think you should have contacted him.'

'I shall send word to Mr Stokes. My man of business can inform him that the interment has already taken place because Richard's death was a suicide and I had no wish to make this fact public. We can also tell Stanton that I have gone to stay with my family and the house is closed.'

'Good idea. That should settle his nerves and give us a week or so to uncover the truth.'

10

Emma decided she would take a footman with her, as she had no intention of knocking on the doors herself. She was awash with tea and almond biscuits by the time she returned home at five o'clock. On enquiry she discovered that Samuel was still out, and she was disappointed she could not tell him immediately what she had found out.

When on her final morning call, with one Mrs Godden at the house adjacent to Mrs Forsyth, she had made discreet enquiries about her neighbours. Emma had been hard-pressed to keep her excitement hidden and had scarcely known how to continue the conversation without revealing her feelings. Now she would have to contain herself until Samuel returned and she could give him the information.

* ⋆ ⋆

Sam rode up to Darlington & Son, the firm he was seeking, and was unsurprised to find it was around the corner from Capel Court where the new stock exchange was located. No doubt it was easier for the brokers to have their offices close by.

He directed his mount under the archway adjacent to the building and was immediately approached by an ostler. 'Leave your horse with me, sir, and then take the side door. It will lead you directly to the vestibule.'

'I'll not be long. There's no need to untack him.' Sam dismounted and tossed the reins to the waiting groom. As he entered the premises he was struck by its opulence — this was a place where gentlemen of means came to discuss their financial dealings. He was definitely a fish out of water in his country clothes and less-than-gentlemanly accent.

A scrawny elderly cove was sitting

behind a desk against the left-hand wall, a giant ledger in front of him. 'Good afternoon, sir. With whom do you have an appointment?'

Sam was about to announce himself as Mr Ashfield, but then realised he would hardly be making investigative enquiries about a complete stranger if he were this person. He would have to revert to his Bow Street Runner name. 'I'm Sergeant Ross from Bow Street. I would like to speak to the person who recently communicated with Mr Richard Stanton of Whitford Hall.'

'I believe that would be young Mr Darlington. If you would care to take a seat, Sergeant Ross, I will make enquiries as to his whereabouts.'

Sam now thought that his appearance was too smart, rather than the reverse. He was fairly sure there wasn't a runner on the books — and there were around four dozen of them — who had togs as good as his. His wits were addled; since he had made the acquaintance of Emma he'd been making elementary mistakes. If he continued in this vein, the whole masquerade would come unravelled before they achieved their objective.

The elderly man returned and almost bowed, but then thought better of it. Sam hid his grin behind his arm as he stood up. His appearance was obviously confusing the clerk. Did he need to come up with an excuse for why he was dressed above his station?

'If you would care to come this way, Sergeant Ross, young Mr Darlington will see you right away.'

Sam was led down an echoing passageway to the rear of the building. The clerk stopped outside an open door. 'Mr Darlington, Sergeant Ross to see you.'

Sam walked into a spacious chamber as well-appointed as the rest of the place. There was obviously money to be made buying and selling bonds and stocks if he was any judge of the matter.

Mr Darlington wasn't sitting behind his desk; he had come round to greet

Sam personally. 'Sergeant. I did not expect Mr Stanton to respond by sending an investigator, but I can see why he would wish to do so. Would you care to take a seat?'

'Before we start, sir, I need to give you the grave news that Mr Stanton was murdered last week. The letter that came from you was no longer in his study, and Lady Emma employed me to find out who killed her husband and what significance your letter had in the tragedy.'

The man staggered forward, and only Sam's quick reflexes prevented him from falling head first against the marble fireplace. 'Dear God! How could this have happened?'

Mr Darlington sagged, and Sam was obliged to heft him like a sack of coal to the nearest chair. He yelled for assistance, and the shrivelled clerk appeared so quickly he must have been lurking outside the door. 'Brandy — fetch it immediately.' The clerk didn't argue, but scuttled across the room and removed a decanter and glass from a bureau. He tipped a generous measure out and then hesitated, as if not sure whether to offer it directly to his superior or give it to Sam.

'Here, allow me. Perhaps somebody could provide tea or coffee as well?' Sam had been holding Darlington upright, and he could feel the man's tremors through his hand. Gently he supported him and put the glass to his lips. 'Drink some of this, sir. It will restore you.'

A great deal of the liquid trickled down Mr Darlington's chin, but he managed to swallow enough of the cognac to bring him to his senses. 'Thank you. I am feeling a lot better now. Would you be kind enough to help me to my desk? Leaning on it will give me the necessary support. I fear I shall tip onto my face again sitting here.'

By the time Sam had settled the man, the sound of rattling crockery could be heard approaching the office. A spotty youth staggered in with a tray, closely followed by the clerk. 'Put it over there, boy, and be ready to collect it when the master has finished.'

The tray was placed on the desk, and the clerk fussed over the contents before stepping back and bowing. 'If you require anything else, sir, there is a bell on the shelf you can ring.'

Mr Darlington waved him away. 'Would you be good enough to pour us both a coffee, Sergeant Ross? I see we have plum cake and almond biscuits. I should like some of each if you please.'

Once they were both served, Sam sat opposite and waited expectantly. After a few sips his patience was rewarded.

'I do apologise for my collapse. My constitution is not as robust as I would like, and sudden shocks are not good for my health. The letter I sent to Mr Stanton was to inform him that his half-brother was now in possession of his portfolio. I assumed this transaction had been legitimate; that they had come to some arrangement between themselves. As I am sure you know, Mr

Benedict Stanton was left with very little when their father died, and has always resented this fact.'

'How did you come to know about these shares?' Sam asked.

'When a large block of shares is transferred, word always gets around the brokers at the stock exchange. I was somewhat dismayed that Mr Richard Stanton, my client, had not used me to accomplish the transfer, but another company.'

Sam finished his drink and poured himself a second cup. This gave him a few moments to process this information. 'Would Mr Benedict Stanton not have realised you would contact his brother?'

'Possibly not. From what I know of him, he is of limited intelligence. I take it these funds were fraudulently transferred?'

'They were. One of the senior partners at the Chelmsford lawyers orchestrated it. Mrs Stanton wouldn't have known, if her husband had not died so suddenly. She only contacted Mr Dickens to inform him of the death, and the theft was discovered then.'

'Can you prove that Mr Richard Stanton did not in fact agree to this transfer? Surely his signature would have been needed?'

'Mr Dickens had signed letters,' Sam explained, 'but they were obviously forgeries. However, the fact that the partner concerned has conveniently resigned his post and moved away makes it difficult to prove. I'm investigating the matter on Lady Emma's behalf, and will let you know what I unearth.'

He spent a further half-hour with Mr Darlington before taking his leave, after which he collected his horse and set out for Tavistock Place. On the ride back he had plenty of time to mull over what he had heard. He realised now that the murder had been intentional; with Richard Stanton dead, his half-brother must believe his crime would never be detected, and that a defenceless widow would accept what had happened, leaving him to live in luxury at her expense. This made it even more urgent that he and Emma somehow obtain an invitation to the party. At the moment, Sam was still at a loss as to how to achieve this; but he had every faith in Collins, and was hopeful his man would come up with a solution.

He could hardly credit that Mr Stanton's fortune had been purloined so easily. If Sam himself had owned even a fraction of that wealth, he would have made damn sure he could account for every penny. He was not looking forward to telling Emma what he'd discovered. The fact that her relationship with her husband had been platonic would not make it any easier for her to accept that Richard Stanton's death had been deliberately orchestrated by his half-brother. Maybe he would leave it until after their guests had departed — better not to upset her before then.

* * *

Emma had spoken to the butler and instructed him to ask Sam to come to see her immediately upon his return. She positioned herself at the far end of the drawing room so that when he eventually turned up, they would not be overheard.

After pacing the carpet for a while, she gravitated towards the pianoforte. She loved to play; it had been her solace and joy in her sterile marriage. There was no need for her to search out a music sheet, for she knew several pieces by heart. She settled herself on the piano stool and began to play a sonata by Schubert, soon becoming lost in the notes.

As the final chords died away, she became aware she was no longer alone. Sam was lounging against the wall and could have been there for some time. He straightened and walked towards her.

'That was superb. I've rarely had the

opportunity to hear anyone play, but even someone as ignorant as I am recognises that you have talent.'

She closed the lid and stood up, inordinately pleased by his compliment. 'Thank you. I have had more than enough time to practise over the past five years. I am so glad you have joined me, as I have something of the utmost importance to tell you.'

Sam followed her to the French doors and they stepped out together onto the terrace. 'My final call was at the house of Mrs Godden,' Emma continued. 'She lives to the right of Mr and Mrs Forsyth. I was the last visitor, and we were alone together, so I was able to make discreet enquiries about those people. It seems that Mr and Mrs Forsyth have given notice on their house and they are moving at the end of the week. They will be sacrificing a great deal of money, according to Mrs Godden, as they have paid for a year's lease in advance. Mrs Godden is worried that undesirables will move in, thus lowering the tone of the neighbourhood. The place will now be left unoccupied until the expiry of the year that has been prepaid.'

'Did she know why they are leaving in such a hurry?'

'One of the remaining outside men is walking out with her kitchen maid, and through this liaison she has discovered they are leaving London because Mr Forsyth has unexpectedly inherited a large sum of money.'

'The more we hear about Mr Forsyth, the more I'm convinced they're directly involved in our investigation. For that man to have gained his wealth at the same time as Stanton is too much of a coincidence.'

This news was not good, and Emma knew there was little time left if they wished to discover the truth and bring Benedict Stanton to justice. 'It is even more imperative that we somehow acquire an invitation to this party, but I am at a loss to know how we are going to achieve this.'

Sam's smile made her catch her breath. 'If necessary, we will gatecrash and hope for the best. There are more than fifty couples invited that we know about; I doubt that an extra pair would be noticed by the staff. After all, they can hardly be loyal retainers, as the bastard has only moved into Cavendish Square recently.'

'What about the fact that Mr and Mrs Forsyth are about to leave the area? If he is indeed the actual murderer, surely we need to know his whereabouts?' For some reason Sam's profanities no longer offended her as they had once done.

He nodded. 'I'll send Collins to Bow Street and ask Mr Fletcher to get a constable to follow them when they move. Did you discover exactly when they're intending to go?'

'At the beginning of next week. Does this mean they are remaining in Town in order to attend the party?'

'Probably. I should be happier if they were not doing so, as I've no wish to take you into danger.' His expression was formidable, and Emma's heart flipped with fear. Suddenly the enormity of her situation overwhelmed her. Her husband Richard had been cruelly murdered, and she and Samuel were intending to confront the perpetrators. Unexpected tears trickled down her cheeks and she turned away quickly, hoping to hide them, but she was too late.

'God dammit to hell! Don't cry, sweetheart. I'll keep you safe.' Sam closed the gap between them and put his arms around her. For a moment she resisted, then relaxed into his embrace. This was the first time in her life she had experienced comfort in another person's arms, and she revelled in the sensation. When he suggested they move, she nodded, too emotional to speak.

He kept his arm firmly around her waist and guided her to a sofa. Still holding her, he gently pulled her down so she was almost in his lap. 'This is madness. I should never have agreed to your suggestion and involved you in this investigation. You're a lady; you should be at Whitford Hall, not living here with me.'

His words cleared her head as nothing else could have done. She sat up and glared at him. 'If you are thinking of sending me back, you can forget about it right now. I was not crying because I am too feeble to continue, but . . . botheration, I've no idea why I've become a watering pot.'

Sam was staring at her in a most peculiar way. A hectic flush crept along his cheekbones and his eyes appeared to darken. A wave of heat spread from Emma's face to her nether regions, and without conscious thought she swayed towards him. One of his hands cupped the back of her head, and with the other he pulled her so close that her breasts were crushed against his chest. Then his mouth closed over hers and she forgot everything. She was lost to a sensation she did not recognise, had never experienced before, and her lips parted of their own volition to allow his hot tongue entry.

Then he lifted her away and vanished through the French doors without another word. Had her wanton behaviour offended him? What had just happened between them? Her lips were tingling, her bodice was unaccountably tight, and she was filled with a strange, unsettling longing. Never in all her life had she imagined that being kissed could be so pleasurable. Samuel should not have taken liberties, but she was glad that he had. He had opened a door to a world she had thought denied to her forever, and she was determined to find out more about this matter before they went their separate ways.

Slowly Emma regained her feet. She could hear Sam striding up and down the terrace like a man possessed. Was it possible he thought he would be dismissed for kissing her? Under normal circumstances, a man in his position could be flogged for putting his hands on a lady such as herself. Why was she not incensed with his behaviour?

Her knees buckled beneath her and she collapsed onto the sofa again. There could be only one reason for her lack of decorum, and that was so outlandish she could hardly believe it. Somehow she had fallen irrevocably in love with a totally unsuitable man.

11

Sam shot out through the door as if pursued by a regiment of Frenchies. What had possessed him to kiss Emma? If she complained, he would be dismissed. Worse than that — quite possibly he would be put before the magistrates. He had ruined everything, thrown his promising career away, and all for what?

There were plenty of light-skirts only too willing to oblige when he felt the need. Yet here he was with his head in the noose because he had let his lust overrule his common sense. This was the best employment he'd had since leaving the army two years ago, and now he'd thrown it all away. In a sense he'd begun to believe the play-acting was real; that she was his wife and not Lady Emma Stanton.

Should he go in and make a

grovelling apology, and pray that she didn't report him? He doubted if she would want to work with him anymore. This was a total disaster, and it was all his fault. He should have known better than to allow his emotions to become involved in a case.

'Samuel, are you upset with me? Should I not have responded to your embrace?'

He stopped so suddenly that his toes jammed against the ends of his boots, almost tipping him onto his nose. He spun round, and for a moment his words were trapped behind his teeth. She wasn't angry, but concerned about her own behaviour.

He stared at her, and it was as if he saw her clearly for the first time. Without conscious thought, he had become overly fond of her, and it would appear that she reciprocated his feelings. A rush of pure joy pumped through him, and for a heady moment he actually believed there could be a future for them together.

Then harsh reality took hold. What-ever her feelings, they could never act on them. Sam was a member of the lower orders and Emma was an aristocrat. Occasionally a toff took a bride beneath his touch, but it would be unheard of for a lady to do the same. She would be ostracised, and any children they had would never be able to find their place in society. They would be neither fish nor fowl, and their lives would be miserable because of it.

Sam knew he must be strong and keep his feelings to himself or it would be the ruin of both of them. He bowed deeply and straightened, almost clicking his heels together in the military fashion. 'It is I who must most humbly beg your pardon, my lady. For a moment I forgot we were play-acting, and that was unforgivable. I give you my word as a man of honour that I will never offend you in such a way again.'

Instead of looking pleased by his apology, Emma pursed her lips and all but stamped her foot. 'Don't be ridiculous, Samuel. You would not have kissed me if I had not encouraged you.' She stared at him, her magnificent eyes sparkling with emotion. 'I am a widow; I answer to no man. I do not have to seek permission or approval for my behaviour. If I wish to . . . to become closer to you, then it's my decision.'

He'd wanted to remain aloof, but could no longer do so. He moved closer and took her smooth white hands between his work-roughened palms. 'You haven't thought this through, my love. There can be no relationship between us — you're the daughter of an earl and I a man wanted for murder. Even if I weren't beneath your touch, it would still be impossible. I've no intention of involving you in my problems. Once this matter has been completed, we'll go our separate ways. You might be sad for a week or two, but will soon realise we made the right decision.'

Emma smiled, and his resolve began

to weaken. 'Fiddlesticks to that. I have spent the past five years being a dutiful wife, and look where that got me. I want to hold a baby in my arms; want to sleep beside the man I love. I care not for society's rules. Are you so feeble-hearted that you will not take a chance on having a happy life with me?'

The suggestion was quite outrageous, but Sam loved her for it. 'We cannot become man and wife because the ceremony would be invalid, as I cannot use my actual name. Do you want any children we have to be bastards?'

'Please, Samuel, let us sit down and talk about this sensibly.' Emma backed towards the sofa, and as he did not release her hands he was obliged to follow. When they were safely settled, she resumed her attack. 'We could be married somewhere in the country where neither of us is known. You could use your real name and I mine, and I doubt that anyone else will ever be the wiser.' As he was still looking unconvinced, she continued. 'Then we could remain Mr and Mrs Ashfield. I have no intention of ever seeing my family again, and you cannot see yours — so we shall start afresh together.' There was a strange glitter in his eyes. Surely those were not tears she could see?

'You would give up everything for me? I can't believe what you're saying — it makes no sense. I'm a murderer and a common soldier. I've no manners and little education.'

Emma raised her hand. 'Stop right now, my love. I care not about your past; it is your future that I want. I've never felt this way in my entire life. I am quite dizzy with happiness, and refuse to give you up.'

Slowly he raised her hands to his mouth and kissed each knuckle in turn. The touch of his lips on her skin was almost too much to bear. 'I hadn't intended to fall in love with you, but it's too late to repine,' he murmured. 'I can only see this ending badly for both of us, but for the moment we'll pretend there is a future for us.'

Emma's head was spinning — it was impossible to think clearly when he was so close. She snatched her hands away and jumped up as he had done earlier. 'You must obtain a special licence, and we will find an obliging vicar to marry us.'

He did not look too pleased at being given orders. His eyes narrowed and his lips thinned, and for a moment Emma wondered if she were making a mistake. Samuel was not like Richard; he would not allow her free rein to please herself but expect her to do as he said. Was she prepared to give up her independence for this man? Her heart thumped uncomfortably, and she was tempted to flee, but she stood her ground. She trusted him. However angry he became, he would never do her actual harm.

Sam towered above her and then pounced, snatching her from her feet. In an instant his mouth covered hers, his lips hard and demanding. His passion almost overwhelmed her. When he put her down, her knees folded beneath her and she slowly subsided into an elegant heap at his feet. He made no attempt to help, but merely stared down at her, his expression inscrutable. Was this some sort of test of her resolve?

She held out her hand imperiously. 'Kindly help me to my feet, sir, and do not stand there gawping down at me like a village idiot.' This was hardly conciliatory speech, but it did the trick. He reached down and grabbed her by her elbows, then lifted her as if she were no heavier than a bag of feathers.

'You're a saucy minx. Being married to you will be a severe strain on my patience.'

Emma couldn't keep back her squeal of joy. 'I love you, Samuel, and I promise that you will have no regrets.' She tilted her head and peeked provocatively from beneath her eyelashes. 'However, I cannot promise that I'll always be dutiful and submissive — I've had my own way for far too long.'

He was still holding her elbows and shoved her unceremoniously onto the sofa. Then he dropped to one knee. 'I suppose I'd better do this properly, or no doubt you'll complain for the next ten years.'

They were hardly the words of a devoted swain, but they made Emma laugh. She sat up straight and clasped her hands in her lap as if she were indeed a young miss about to receive her first offer.

'Emma, would you do me the honour of becoming my wife, even if we do have to marry and then live under assumed names?'

'I should be delighted to marry you, and care not how we are called as long as we are man and wife.'

Sam sprung to his feet, his face was alight with laughter and love. Emma didn't care how unsuitable he was; that if her unpleasant family were ever to hear of her mésalliance, they would have it annulled. She was going to marry the man she loved, and no one and nothing would stop her.

'How long have we got before we must change for dinner?' Sam asked her.

She glanced at the overmantel clock. 'An hour at least. Plenty of time to discuss the details and problems we might encounter because of our decision.'

He flopped down beside her and slid his arm around her waist; she rested her head on his shoulder. A wave of happiness engulfed her — for the first time she knew what it was like to be loved and to be able to love back.

'What happens to Whitford Hall when you marry me? If we are to keep our nuptials secret, how can I run the estate for you?'

'Stokes is running the estate at the moment,' Emma answered. 'I shall get him to move into the house and bring his wife and children with him. We must take him into our confidence — as indeed we must with any of the staff we intend to keep — and he shall take care of things until my father is dead and can no longer interfere in my life. I shall ask him to give us two-thirds of the profits so that we have sufficient to live on. Any sons that we might be blessed with will be able to take over the estate when they reach their majority.'

'Yes, I think that might work. What about Stanton? Do you not think he might kick up a dust if you disappear? I think it likely he'll have you declared deceased or incompetent, and seize the estate for himself.'

She snuggled closer, and almost forgot what she had been going to say as the heat from his body seeped through the thin muslin of her afternoon gown. 'You are forgetting, my love, that we intend to expose him as the villain that he is. He will either be incarcerated or exiled, and in no position to object to anything we might do.' Something important occurred to her, but she could not think straight when she was in his arms. Much to his amusement, she sat up and moved to the far end of the sofa. 'Things are becoming clearer to me as we talk,' she continued. 'Although we shall be married as soon as we can, once Stanton is dealt with I shall return to Whitford Hall and live in my former persona until we have the stolen funds returned to us. Only then will we leave and begin our new life as Mr and Mrs Ashfield.'

Sam raised an eyebrow in a most annoying way and shook his head sadly as if she were talking fustian. 'I can see one snag with your plan, my darling. What if you were with child? I hardly think that would improve your standing in the community.'

Her cheeks burned hot at the thought of what would have to take place in order for her to be in an interesting condition. He was barely suppressing his mirth at her discomfiture. Being laughed at was a new experience, and not one she particularly enjoyed.

'Thank you so much for pointing out the flaw in my reasoning, my dear,' she said. 'The solution is obvious — we shall not consummate our union until this matter is concluded.'

Sam's expression changed, and she recognised the warning signal as skipped nimbly out of his reach and dashed for the exit. He was quicker and slammed his hands on either side of her, trapping her against his hard frame and the door.

'If you think I'll wait a second longer than I have to, sweetheart, then you don't know me very well. Ever since I met you — I cannot believe it's only ten days ago — I've wanted to make love to you. You're the most beautiful woman I've ever set eyes on.'

She was finding it difficult to breathe. His distinctive aroma of sweat and lemon soap made her head swim. She wanted to share her body with him, but knew she must not until they were united in the sight of God. She raised her hands, placed them flat on his chest, and gently pushed. To her surprise, he allowed himself to be moved back.

'Then, Samuel my love, you must

purchase a special licence and we shall be married as soon as you have it.'

His breathing was as laboured as hers, and she revelled in the fact that she was able to do this to him. What they were planning was dangerous and could easily end in disaster for both of them, but she was prepared to risk everything for this man.

'I've no idea how to go about such a task,' he said, 'but will find out tomorrow. Have you any idea what we do once I have the licence in my possession?'

'I believe that all we have to do is find a willing priest and two witnesses, and then we can be married anytime and anywhere, though perhaps I am wrong.'

'I think I'll ask Benton. We'll have to take him into our confidence anyway.'

Sam was gone for less than a quarter of an hour, and returned looking worried. 'I don't know why your husband's old valet should know such things, but he does. In order to obtain a licence, we have to prove we have resided in the parish for three weeks or more, and then we must marry within that parish and in a church.'

'Then that is what we will do. We cannot marry where I am known, so we will remain here until we have fulfilled the residential requirements. Was Benton shocked by your enquiry?'

Sam grinned, which made him look younger and more approachable. 'Far from it — he actually smiled at me. I don't anticipate any problems with the staff you brought from Whitford Hall; they will keep our secret.'

'You know, my love, that for the first time in my life I am truly happy. I had a miserable childhood — I was regularly beaten and allowed no pleasures at all. Marrying Richard was the first and only time I rebelled; and despite the strangeness of our relationship, he offered me a safe home after years of misery.'

'I promise that I'll make you happy, my darling, and that you'll never regret your decision.'

They settled back onto a convenient sofa, and she snuggled into his arms.

'You know, Samuel, I no longer mind if we never bring Benedict Stanton to justice. Indeed, if it were not for the fact that I should like to recover the money he stole so we can have a comfortable life for ourselves and our children, I would suggest that we abandon our quest.'

He kissed the top of her head. 'I know what you mean, but I intend to bring this matter to a satisfactory conclusion. This will be my last case as Sergeant Ross, and I want to leave the Bow Street Runners with my record of success intact.'

The overmantel clock struck the hour and Emma sighed. 'We must change for dinner, my love. Our guests will be here within the hour.'

12

Mr and Mrs Waters proved to be convivial guests. He was a down-to-earth businessman, and she a lady of middle years with too much time on her hands. When Emma took her guest into the drawing room, leaving the men to their port, she was looking forward to conversing with another woman.

Over the years she had been starved of female conversation, as Richard had not encouraged her to make morning calls or meet any of the neighbouring families. Mrs Waters was petite, her fair hair untouched by grey, and her figure would be the envy of a woman half her age. Although not dressed in the height of fashion, her garments were elegant and well-made.

'I have enjoyed this evening, Mrs Ashfield. I do thank you for inviting us. This is the first time I have accompanied Mr Waters on a business trip, and was finding it decidedly tedious been cooped up on my own all day in our rented accommodation.'

'I am delighted that you came,' Emma said. 'I too was feeling the lack of female company. Mr Ashfield and I have not been married long, and I was unable to make any attachments before as I had the care of my ailing parents.' She was shocked at how easily these lies tripped from her tongue. 'My father died two years ago, and my mother the following year. Mr Ashfield and I had been known to each other for some time.'

'My dear Mrs Ashfield, there's no need to tell me more. I can see yours is a love match. It seems so long ago since my wedding and when I too felt the same way. Do not misunderstand me — I am sincerely attached to him; but since our three children have flown the nest, we have little to say to each other.'

'Do you know anything of a Mr Benedict Stanton?' Emma spoke without thought, immediately wishing she could retract her question.

'Indeed we do. He used to lodge nearby. Recently he came into an inheritance and has gone up in the world. It's quite extraordinary you should mention his name, as only the other day we received an invitation to attend a soirée at his new address in Cavendish Square. Unfortunately we cannot go, as we are travelling to St Albans on that day to visit my eldest daughter.'

'We have discovered that Mr Stanton is distantly related to my husband,' Emma lied, 'and would dearly like to make his acquaintance, as we do not have any other family that we know of.'

'That wish is easily granted, Mrs Ashfield. You must have our invitation. I very much doubt that Mr Stanton would even remember us. Indeed, I cannot imagine why he felt it necessary to invite us in the first place.'

The gentlemen had joined them and Mr Waters overheard his wife's remark. 'Mr Stanton invited us, my dear, because I was able to do him a favour or two when he was without funds. He repaid me in full when he gained his wealth, and I believe this invitation is another way for him to show his gratitude.'

'If you are sure you will not be going to the party, then we would be delighted to attend in your place,' Emma said.

'Have you visited the menagerie at the Tower, Mrs Ashfield?' Mrs Waters asked eagerly.

'I have not, but would dearly like to do so; if you are not busy we could go tomorrow. At what time shall I call for you?'

'I find it difficult to sleep with all the racket going on in the street outside, so the earlier the better for me.'

'I shall be there at ten o'clock. Perhaps we could visit Gunter's and have an ice before we return? Mr Ashfield treated me the other day and I found it quite delicious.'

'Then that is agreed, Mrs Ashfield. I

shall give you the invitation when we meet tomorrow morning.'

The remainder of the evening passed pleasantly enough; Emma played for them and they were suitably impressed. After the tea tray had been removed, Mr and Mrs Waters took their leave.

'That was most enjoyable,' Emma said to Sam. 'I've never hosted a dinner party before and was somewhat nervous about doing so. Did you enjoy yourself, Samuel?'

'I did indeed, sweetheart. Mr and Mrs Waters are good company. This evening was as new to me as it was to you. People of my ilk don't attend dinner parties or sit around chit-chatting over the tea tray afterwards.'

'I'll hear no more of that talk, my love. From now on we are equals. I am no longer a titled lady, and you are now a gentleman. Have you given any thought to where we might settle after your investigation is completed?'

'It can't be anywhere near St Albans, Chelmsford or London in case we're recognised. Where does your father live?'

'In Surrey, near Guildford. My brother also has his principal estate in that county. I have heard that Norwich, in Norfolk, is a pleasant place to live. Shall we go there?'

'It's as good a place as any as far as I'm concerned. I've not visited the city myself, but have heard positive reports. It's a thriving business centre despite being so far from London.'

'We have a further week to wait before we are eligible to marry, and the party is not until Saturday. Shall we venture down there and see for ourselves?' Emma suggested. 'I believe one can travel by coach all the way. We would have to overnight en route in each direction.'

Sam yawned loudly and then dropped a swift kiss on her parted lips. 'We shall visit Norwich once we're married, sweetheart. I've no wish to pre-empt our wedding night, and that would be inevitable if I were obliged to share a room with you.'

She flushed hot all over at his comment. 'In which case, we shall go after the party. You are obviously tired, my dear, so I think it's time we said good night.'

They strolled arm in arm from the terrace and up the stairs, only parting on the landing. 'I love you, Emma Stanton,' Sam declared, 'and give you my word as a newly fledged gentleman that I'll make you far happier than you have been the past five years.'

She stood on tiptoe in order to kiss him. 'I know I shouldn't say so, but since Richard died and you came into my life I've discovered what happiness is. My so-called friends and family would be shocked to the core that I am not wearing widow's weeds and grieving for Richard, but I care not what they think. From now on that life is over and I am a new woman, free to love and live as I please.'

Sam watched her until she disappeared into her own apartment before returning downstairs. He wasn't ready to retire. Collins would have information to give him, and now was the ideal time.

Foster was waiting to speak to him when he reached the vestibule. 'If you could spare me a few moments of your time, Mr Ashfield, I should be grateful.'

Sam gestured towards the study and the butler followed him. He wasn't sure if he should offer the cove a chair or keep him standing, but decided the elderly gentleman deserved to sit, even if it breached etiquette. 'How can I help you, Foster?'

'This is a delicate subject, Mr Ashfield, but I must speak of it.' He shifted uncomfortably on his chair and looked around the room before raising his eyes. 'I'm afraid that your secret is discovered, sir. A tradesman recognised you.'

'Exactly what do you believe my secret is, Foster?' The man looked more uncomfortable than accusatory, so maybe he had only got half the story.

'You are not a businessman from the

country, but an investigator from Bow Street. You and your wife are using an assumed name.'

'You're right in your assumptions,' Sam admitted. 'Bringing my wife along is excellent cover.'

'We knew Mr and Mrs Forsyth were not what they appeared, and we're not surprised you've been sent to look into matters. Will you be leaving as soon as your enquiries are complete?'

Now matters became clearer to Sam. The staff were worried they would be without employment; they cared little for the reason he and Emma were actually living there. 'I'm hoping to complete my investigation by next week,' Sam told him. 'However, my wife has spent little time in London and wishes to remain here until the lease is up. I lodge in Covent Garden when I'm working, and she remains at our home in Romford.'

As he told these lies his mind was racing. Wouldn't the butler think it strange that he could afford two homes, however modest?

Instead of looking sceptical, Foster nodded. 'We hoped that might be the case, sir, and I am relieved to hear you confirm it. I can give you my word that your secret is safe with us. The butcher who was delivering here when he spotted you won't say a word; he values our custom too much.'

'I'm glad this matter has been sorted out to our mutual satisfaction,' Sam said. 'It's vital that Mr and Mrs Forsyth don't know I'm watching them. Forsyth is suspected of murder and grand larceny, and I believe my investigations are nearing a satisfactory conclusion. I hope to apprehend Mr Forsyth before he leaves the area.'

He stood up and Foster scrambled to his feet. 'I bid you good evening, sir, and wish you good luck in your task.'

No sooner had the butler gone than Collins appeared. 'It's damned late; I'm sorry to have kept you waiting,' Sam apologised. 'Sit down, man — we've a lot to discuss.' Sam told him Foster's news and he was unsurprised. He was equally unmoved by the announcement that his employer was going to move to Norwich under an assumed name, and marry a member of the aristocracy. However, he sat up and took notice when Sam told him about having obtained an invitation to the party.

'I'm not sure that you should take Mrs Ashfield, sir. I reckon that the butcher isn't the only one who might have recognised you. I've noticed a couple of rum coves drifting around the back of this house the past couple of days. One of them is employed by Mr Forsyth.'

'Even if they have recognised me, they can't possibly know the identity of the woman pretending to be my wife,' Sam said. 'Neither will they know about the invitation. We're unlikely to meet up with any of Forsyth's minions at such a grand event.'

'Stanton's hiring extra staff for the night, so I thought I'd get myself a job as an ostler; I'm not likely to cut it as an indoor man. If you and Mrs Ashfield are going to be inside, you're going to need somebody in there with you. Stanton and Forsyth have got too much to lose and wouldn't hesitate to murder both of you if you were discovered poking about where you shouldn't be.'

If Collins hadn't looked so earnest, Sam would have laughed. 'I take your point, and thank you for your concern. As the staff are well aware of my masquerade, I think I'll send a couple of the footmen round and see if they can get themselves a temporary post. Do you know the name of the agency handling this?'

His man dug into his waistcoat pocket and produced a grubby piece of paper. 'Got it down here, sir. I thought you might want to use it. I'll nip down to the servants' hall now, shall I? Reckon as they might still be up.'

Whilst Collins was gone, Sam had time to gather his thoughts. When Emma had suggested she join him in London, it had seemed like a sensible notion, but now that had all changed. Being in love with her meant he was reluctant to expose her to any kind of risk, and he would kill without hesitation any man or woman who offered her harm.

★   ★   ★

When Emma came down the next morning she was immediately aware that the house felt different. At first she couldn't put a finger on the change; but when the parlourmaid put her morning chocolate on the table beside her with a conspiratorial smile, she understood. Somehow the staff had become privy to their secret. Instead of being shocked or judgemental, however, they appeared to believe themselves part of the dissembling.

'Is Mr Ashfield in the house?' Emma asked.

The girl bobbed and nodded. 'Yes, Mrs Ashfield. He's in the study. I took a tray in a while ago.'

'Then I shall eat my breakfast in the study with my husband. Kindly bring me toast and marmalade as well as my chocolate.'

The maid didn't smirk at this remark, but merely smiled and rushed away with the chocolate. Emma paused outside the study to knock and was relieved to be bid to enter immediately. The maid arrived behind her with the tray and Emma stood to one side to allow her to take it in.

'Please put it on the desk. That will be all for now, thank you.'

Samuel was munching his way through an enormous plate of fried ham and mushrooms. He finished his mouthful and gestured with his fork for Emma to sit down beside him. He waited until the door closed behind the parlourmaid before speaking. 'I'm glad you're here, sweetheart. There have been developments you need to know of.'

'I've guessed that the staff know we are not who we say. You must explain the whole to me.'

When he had finished, she was relieved she had not been unmasked as Lady Emma Stanton, but was concerned that Mr Forsyth possibly knew Samuel was from Bow Street. 'I shall be glad when this week is over and we have concluded this investigation one way or another,' she said. 'If we are unable to find the proof we need on Saturday, Samuel, will you give me your word you will let the matter rest? I fear that if we poke about too much, our deceit will be revealed, and the first person to hear about it would be my father.' Her breakfast threatened to return at the very idea the earl might come back into her life and destroy her newfound happiness.

'Don't look like that, my dear. I promise you no one will hurt you, not even that bastard. Whatever happens on Saturday, we shall be married before the earl has time to interfere.'

'You don't know what it's like,' Emma pressed. 'He would ruin both of us. You can be very sure it wouldn't be long before he discovered the reason you have been calling yourself Samuel Ross these past ten years. Then you would hang, and I would be a widow again — but this time with no claim to the Stanton money. I would be entirely at my father's mercy.'

'We'll be long gone before that happens,' Sam insisted. 'Although I've told the staff here that we intend to remain for the duration of our lease, I'm putting plans in motion for us to make a hasty escape as soon as we're wed, just in case it's necessary.'

'That reminds me — under what name has Benton gone this morning to acquire the special licence?'

'Under my true name. I suppose I'd better tell you what it is. You're about to become Mrs Samuel Rutherford, my darling. As I killed that man more than ten years ago, I'm hoping such a common name as Rutherford will not arouse alarm bells at the bishop's palace.'

'Then we shall be known as Mr and Mrs Rutherford when we move to Norfolk.' Emma paused before continuing. 'I've been thinking about my suggestion that we find out how your family fared after you fled. I think it probably wiser if we send Collins to make enquiries and not go ourselves.' She tilted her head on one side and pursed her lips. 'You might be ten years older, but I doubt anyone will have forgotten what you look like. You are a head taller than most men, and with such a striking appearance you will have made an impression on more than one young lady.'

'There you're wrong, sweetheart, for I've grown half a head since I left Hertfordshire and must weigh twice as much. You forget, I was still a half-grown stripling when it happened. I think it unlikely even my own parents would recognise me now. My face is battered and scarred from my time on the Peninsular, and my hair, for some unfathomable reason, is much darker than it was when I was seventeen years of age.'

'That's good news indeed, for it makes it far less likely anyone will ever recognise you or link your name with that of the under-groom from Hertfordshire.'

The tall-case clock in the corner of the room struck the hour. Emma dropped her cutlery and jumped to her feet in horror. 'Good grief! I'm supposed to be picking up Mrs Waters in half an hour and I've yet to put on my bonnet. Samuel, could you please ensure the carriage is waiting when I come down in five minutes' time?'

He nodded. 'I've managed to obtain a set of plans for the house in which Stanton is now living, which I intend to study this morning and make sure I'm familiar with the layout of the house before we go there on Saturday. I'm not sure that you should come, Emma; it might be extremely dangerous.'

'But you need me there. You're not yet equipped to mingle with the *ton*,

213

and would be exposed as an impostor immediately.' She said this as she reached the door. His reply echoed in her ears as she ran off.

'And you might well be recognised as Lady Emma Stanton — and then we'll set up someone's bristles right enough.'

13

Mrs Waters proved again to be an entertaining companion; and although considerably older than herself, Emma believed she might have found someone who would become a close friend. The menagerie proved to be a disappointment, however, as neither of them enjoyed the spectacle of wild animals being penned in small metal cages.

'I am quite exhausted and hungry, Mrs Waters,' Emma said. 'I believe I shall have more than an ice at Gunter's today. They have excellent cake available. Shall we have some?'

Her companion agreed. 'I should like to have a cup of coffee and some cake first, and then we can wander around Berkeley Square eating our ice creams. I know that we'll outrage the tabbies, but as it's unlikely we'll ever see them again, I don't give a fig for their opinion.'

This was refreshing talk indeed. 'You're right, Mrs Waters. We ladies spend far too much time worrying about the rules and conventions of society in general. We can be as scandalous as we wish — nobody knows who we are, and we shall be gone from Town in a few weeks' time.'

'That's the spirit, Mrs Ashfield. I have no aspirations to be part of the ruling classes. We are firmly in the middle — *bourgeoisie*, if you like — and I believe that people of our sort can lead a far more interesting life than those above us.'

Emma was tempted to tell her the truth but thought better of it. As the carriage rattled across the cobbles towards Gunter's, she was having second thoughts. 'I think that as I am intending to take your place at Mr Stanton's party on Saturday, maybe it would be sensible not to draw attention to ourselves today. It would be a horrible coincidence if someone attending the party happened to be in Berkeley Square, but I think we should not take the risk.'

'I hadn't thought of that, my dear, and you're quite correct. We must be circumspect today. However, next week we must throw our bonnets over the windmill and go out of our way to break the rules.'

'That sounds like an excellent notion. When do you return to Town from your visit to your daughter's home in St Albans?'

'We are not making a long stay and should be in London again the following week. I shall expect to hear all about the party and whether or not you managed to introduce yourselves to your long-lost cousin.'

Emma swallowed a lump in her throat. It was perfectly possible that circumstances might prevent her from meeting Mrs Waters again. She prayed that would not be the case and forced herself to smile brightly. 'It's possible we will be away from London for a while, but I promise that as soon as Mr Ashfield and I are back in residence I'll send a note round, and we shall get together.'

The visit to Gunter's was as enjoyable as Emma had expected, and the cake quite delicious. She was sad to say farewell to her new friend and vowed she would continue the acquaintance if she could. The invitation to Benedict Stanton's house-warming party was safely in her reticule. Her part done for the moment, it was now up to Samuel and his colleagues to take the matter forward.

He was waiting to greet her when she walked into the drawing room. 'Did you enjoy your excursion, my love?' he asked her.

'I did indeed. Mrs Waters is quite delightful.' She held out the invitation she had retrieved from her reticule. 'Here you are. I think it appropriate that you have this. Shall we walk around the garden for a while? It's far too clement to remain indoors.'

Sam took the card, but instead of putting it in his pocket he walked across to the mantel shelf and tucked it behind the clock. 'Don't look so worried,

Emma. I doubt that either of the parlourmaids will read it. Anyway, all the staff are well aware we're not who we say we are.'

The garden was in full sunlight and she decided she would prefer to sit in the shade on the terrace. Once she was comfortably settled, he joined her.

'Benton has the licence and has also found the ideal church in which we can be wed,' Sam said. 'We shall have fulfilled the residential requirements by next week, and the ceremony will take place at eleven o'clock next Wednesday.'

'Have you thought who can stand as witnesses? Benton obviously, and perhaps Collins could be the second?'

'I agree. It makes no difference to me as long as we're legally married. Collins, an under-groom and the two footmen have obtained positions for the day of the party, which means I shall have two men outside and two in. It's possible that Forsyth and his wife will be guests; but his henchmen, the men who might have known me, won't be inside. I'm intending to look quite different from my usual appearance.'

'As I've said before, you're too tall to go unrecognised,' Emma said. 'How do you intend to disguise yourself?'

'Benton has it in hand — you'll have to wait until the night to see how changed I'll be. Did you bring a suitable gown for such an occasion?'

'It wouldn't do to look too elegant, Samuel. After all, we are supposed to be Mr and Mrs Waters, are we not?'

He shook his head and leaned across to brush a stray curl from her face. Just the touch of his fingers made her pulse race. 'Whoever is collecting the cards will have no idea which one belongs to which guests once they're inside the building,' he said. 'We'll be mingling with wealthy folk; we need to blend in and not be treated like poor relations.'

It made sense. 'In which case I shall wear the one fine evening gown that I own; I had it made last year but never expected to have the opportunity to wear it.'

They sat in companionable silence while listening to the birds singing and the distant rumble and clatter of the traffic. Emma's hand had moved of its own volition until it was resting in Sam's. This was how things should have been between her and Richard. She should never have made such an impulsive marriage, but the alternative would have been far worse.

'By the by, I took your advice and have sent Collins to make enquiries about my parents. I didn't tell him the whole, but I think he guessed my connection to these Rutherfords. He left as soon as he'd obtained his place for the party; he'll be there and back today.' His fingers tightened over hers.

'I pray he brings you good news. I shall wait up with you until he returns, and play to keep your mind busy.'

'Thank you; I'll look forward to that. Now, sweetheart, I believe I see the butler hovering anxiously. It must be almost time for dinner.'

Emma scrambled to her feet. 'I am

still wearing my promenade gown. Small wonder Foster is becoming agitated. Even in such a household as ours, it would never do for the mistress to be seen at dinner dressed this way.'

★ ★ ★

Although dinner was delicious, neither of them did it justice. Every time there were footsteps outside the drawing room, they both tensed.

'I've told Foster to bring Collins here as soon as he arrives.' Samuel glanced at his watch. 'Are you sure you don't want to retire, sweetheart? It's after eleven o'clock. I can't think why Collins hasn't come; it has been dark for an hour.'

'Shall we give him until midnight and then go up? He must have overnighted somewhere. I'm sure there is nothing untoward about his tardiness.'

There was no need for Sam to reply, as Collins arrived at that moment. He was dust-spattered and dishevelled and had not paused to tidy himself. His news must be urgent indeed.

Emma moved closer to Samuel and his hand gripped hers. 'Come in, man,' he said. 'What news do you have?'

Foster appeared behind Collins. 'Shall I bring refreshments, madam?'

'Yes, and then you may retire,' Emma replied. 'Mr Ashfield will lock up for you tonight.'

Samuel had already taken his man by the arm and led him out onto the terrace. Emma hurried after them. Collins was collapsed on a stone bench, apparently unable to talk. The butler staggered in carrying a large laden tray, which he placed on the table. Then with a small bow he vanished, leaving the three of them alone.

'Here, drink this — you look parched.' Samuel handed Collins a pewter mug of small-beer, which the man downed in two gulps. He wiped his mouth with his sleeve.

'My, that was good. I'd had nothing since I left here this morning.'

'Eat your fill, Collins,' Sam told him. 'We've waited all evening for your news; another few minutes won't hurt.'

'No, Sergeant. I've been that excited to tell you, my meal can wait.' Collins refilled his mug and drained it before continuing. 'You'd better be seated, sir — what I've learned will all but floor you.'

They did as he suggested and waited eagerly for his information. Emma's heart was thudding painfully; from the man's demeanour she was sure the news must be good.

'It's like this, Sergeant,' Collins began. 'It's a right pity you didn't hang around to see what happened after you killed that little bastard. After you did a runner, all hell broke loose, and three other maids came forward and said the same thing had happened to them.'

'God's teeth!' exclaimed Sam. 'I've sometimes regretted killing him, but now I'm glad I did.' He was leaning forward, and even in the gloom Emma could see his excitement.

224

'Well, Lord Frobisher was that horrified his own son could be such a bastard that he was relieved you'd taken the decision from him. The death was called a riding accident, and your pa and ma went up in the world. They searched everywhere for you, and put adverts in the paper; but you'd vanished, and they thought they'd never see you again.'

Samuel was on his feet. 'I must go at once and see them. You must come too, Emma. I can't believe it! All this time, I've been running and hiding for nought.'

'There's more, Sergeant, and it ain't such good news.'

'Go on, Collins. What is it I need to know?'

'Your little sister, Nancy, got a child from her experience. His lordship was prepared to recognise the girl as his granddaughter, but instead your ma is raising it as her own.'

'And my sister — what of her?'

'She's married now and has two little

ones of her own. She moved away to another village so the gossip wouldn't follow her. Mr Rutherford is now the estate manager, and a right big house they live in. They can't wait to see you.' Having completed his tale, Collins tucked into the laden tray.

Emma drew Samuel away so they could talk freely. 'I cannot believe what we have just heard,' she said. 'You can resume your place in the world, and I can become your wife without fear of you being apprehended if ever it became known you were a wanted fugitive.'

'This changes everything, my love. We don't have to be married without family and friends. We can tie the knot at Sandridge Church.'

'Doesn't that mean we will have to apply for another licence?'

'No — I'll speak to the vicar when we go down tomorrow, and he can call the banns on the next three Sundays. It means postponing our nuptials for a week or two, but I think it'll be worth it.

I doubt if your father will get to hear about it; and even if he does, there's nothing he can do to harm us anymore.'

The clatter of cutlery being dropped onto a plate reminded them that Collins was still on the terrace with them. 'I'm off to my bed, Sergeant,' he said. 'Good night, Mrs Ashfield.'

'Good night, Mr Collins. Thank you for completing the journey in a day in order to bring us the good news.'

With a cheery wave that was barely visible in the darkness, he vaulted over the stone balustrade and headed for the gate that led to his accommodation above the stables.

'I shall take the tray inside and leave it in the vestibule, and then I'll retire,' Emma said. 'What time do you wish me to be ready to leave in the morning?'

'We'll go as soon as you're ready,' replied Sam. 'We will need to pack an overnight bag, and I suggest we take your maid and my valet with us. I'll lock up and remove the debris. Good night, sweetheart.'

'Good night, my love. I'll be ready by nine o'clock.'

* * *

Sam took his time tidying and checking that he house was secure. His head was full of amazing possibilities, as for the first time in ten years he was free to come and go as he pleased. Tomorrow he would see his beloved parents again and find out what his youngest sister Mary was doing. She'd been in leading strings when he left, and would be a grown woman by now. There was also the matter of his niece, although he'd better refer to her as his sister. How was he going to feel when he met her? He hoped she didn't look like her natural father, as that would remind him of his killing of the man.

This left the small matter of Emma's ancestry to be considered. It might be better to keep this private, and introduce her as the widow of Richard Stanton. He dumped the tray in the passageway that led to the servants' hall and bounded up the stairs.

Benton was already abed, so Sam couldn't ask him — no, tell him — that he was to accompany his master to St Albans the next morning. Sandridge was a village no more than five miles from the city, and was a place he'd never thought to see again.

As Sam was drifting off to sleep, it occurred to him that he was now known by three different names. The sooner he became plain Mr Rutherford, the happier he'd be. He was done with soldiering and criminal investigations — from now on he wanted to become the gentleman he'd been pretending to be these past three weeks.

* * *

Annie had waited up even though she'd been told she wouldn't be needed any more that night. The girl was bursting with news she couldn't wait to share.

'You'd never guess what's happened,

ma'am,' she said to Emma. 'Mr Benton is getting married next week!'

Emma almost revealed their secret, so great was her shock. 'Are you sure? I've known him for years and he's never shown the slightest interest in matrimony.'

'Mrs Philips overheard him talking to Mr Foster about having got a special licence and having found the perfect church. We can't think who he might be marrying. Do you know, Mrs Ashfield?'

'I've absolutely no idea. I shall ask Mr Ashfield tomorrow. Now, as you're here, I can tell you that we're going away tomorrow to St Albans. I need a valise packed for myself and for you. Mr Ashfield wishes to depart promptly at nine o'clock, so I shall need to be dressed and ready an hour before that time.'

The girl curtsied. 'I'll sort things out before I retire, ma'am. I'll not disturb you in the dressing room.'

This was an unmitigated disaster. Emma could see no way through the muddle that wouldn't involve revealing far too much of their plans. It was one thing for Collins, Foster and Benton to be aware of what was going on, but quite another for the entire staff to know.

She curled up on the window seat in front of the open window, enjoying the cool breeze that drifted in. London in the summer was not nearly as bad as she'd feared — at least, it wasn't for those fortunate enough to be living in such pleasant surroundings.

The majority of the staff knew that she and Samuel were not Mr and Mrs Ashfield, and those who had come with them from Whitford Hall knew her true identity, though the London staff they'd inherited should be ignorant of that fact. But there the problems began. Some of the staff thought she was in fact Samuel's wife brought with him to add depth to his story, but that their name was not Ashfield. Presumably they now thought she was Mrs Ross. The fact that they were now taking

Benton and Annie, plus the grooms and coachmen, to visit Mr and Mrs Rutherford was just adding more complication. It would be impossible to hide Samuel's identity when he would no doubt be greeted like the prodigal son. If Annie, a dreadful gossip, were to discover that Emma and Samuel were getting married as soon as the banns were read, this choice morsel of tittle-tattle would be all over the house, and no doubt the neighbourhood, within hours of their return. And although Emma trusted the loyalty of the staff who had come with them from Whitford Hall, there was grave danger that news of her intended nuptials might somehow reach the earl — or even worse, Benedict Stanton. A careless word spoken to the wrong person, and they would be undone.

She no longer cared about getting her revenge on her brother-in-law. Neither he nor her father would let her marry if they heard about it. Stanton would stand to lose what he considered his rightful inheritance, and the earl and her brother would believe that her marrying a member of the lower classes would place a permanent stain on the family name.

A chill settled in her stomach and her newfound happiness trickled away beneath the weight of what appeared to be insurmountable problems. Less than a month ago she had been the respectable wife of a wealthy gentleman, and now she was a widow about to marry a man she hardly knew. Perhaps it would be more sensible to return to Whitford Hall and pretend that none of this had happened.

14

There was an air of subdued excitement in the house when Emma went down to breakfast, which only served to increase her misgivings about her situation. She had spent a sleepless night mulling over the impossible position she found herself in and could see only one remedy, however heartbreaking that might be.

Her behaviour since Richard had been murdered was disgraceful — she should be at home wearing widow's weeds and acting with circumspection and decorum. As she made her way to the breakfast parlour she came to a decision. The carriage must take her back to Whitford Hall, and Samuel would have to ride to Sandridge on his own. He must also complete his investigation without her assistance.

The only explanation she could give

for her extraordinary behaviour was that anger and grief had turned her head. She had always been a quiet person; had never done anything remotely unladylike. So what had possessed her to gallivant off to London with a Bow Street Runner? Not only that, but somehow she had agreed to marry him. What had she been thinking of?

The letter she had written explaining her decision was clutched in her hand, and she braced herself to enter the breakfast parlour and hand it to Sam. The room was empty, so she checked to see if he was in his study, but that too was deserted. He must be outside, and she could hardly pursue him there. After what had passed between them, she had wished to say her farewells in person, but perhaps it would be better this way.

Foster answered her summons immediately. 'Have the carriage brought round immediately,' she told him. 'I wish to leave now.'

'Mr Ashfield has gone out, madam,

but he assured me he would be back by nine o'clock.'

'I shall be ready to leave in ten minutes.'

There was no time to pack her belongings, so they would have to be sent after her. One thing she was quite certain of — if she did not leave before Samuel returned, she would not leave at all. However much she wished to deny it, she had fallen in love with him, and knew if she allowed him to, he could make her happy.

But she must put her personal wishes to one side and behave as her upbringing had taught her. She was Lady Emma Stanton, a member of the aristocracy. A union with Sergeant Ross was doomed to failure. However much she loved him, he was a poorly educated and rough soldier, more used to mixing with the dregs of society than making polite conversation in a drawing room.

Annie made no comment when she was told they were departing immediately. Where should she put the letter so that Samuel found it upon his return? 'Annie, kindly give this to Benton, and then we are going. Bring the bags with you.'

Part of her wished that Samuel would return early and prevent her leaving, but for both their sakes she knew she had made the right decision. She would never regret having met him; he would always be the man she loved, and she would never marry another even to have children of her own.

She looked neither to the right nor the left as she hurried through the house for the last time, and was glad she had chosen a deep-brimmed bonnet that served to hide her misery from Foster and the footman waiting to assist her into the carriage. As soon as her maid was safely inside with her, Emma banged on the roof. The carriage rocked forward, and she held her breath until they had negotiated the corner and pulled onto the main thoroughfare.

'Annie, tell the coachman to take us to Whitford Hall.'

The girl leant out of the window and shouted up the new instructions, but had the good sense not to query the reason for this precipitous return.

Emma settled into the corner and did her best to keep her tears at bay. This was the right decision, but living without the man she loved was going to be nigh-on impossible. She sniffed and wiped her eyes again. At least she could grieve in public, as everyone would assume her sadness was caused by the untimely death of her husband and not because she was giving up her true love.

The toll road out of London was relatively smooth; and the motion of the carriage, combined with her lack of sleep, caused Emma to doze. She wasn't sure how long she'd been asleep when the carriage lurched violently and stopped, which jerked her to consciousness. For a second she wasn't sure where she was, but then she remembered and her eyes brimmed. She was sniffling into her sodden handkerchief when the door was flung open. Before she could protest, she was lifted bodily from the squabs and sat down none too gently on the grass that edged the road.

'What the hell do you think you're playing at? I should be seeing my parents for the first time in ten years, and instead I've had to gallop across country to fetch you back.'

Emma had never seen Samuel like this. He towered above her, his eyes hard and his expression unfriendly. Something deep inside her had kept a flicker of hope alive that he would come after her and beg her to return. She hadn't considered for a moment that he would be furious with her.

Her words refused to come and it took several long seconds before she was able to respond to his remark. 'I told you in my letter my reasons for leaving. It is not I preventing you from a reunion with your family. You could be there now, rather than here, glaring down at me.'

This was hardly a sensible comment, and further inflamed his anger. He gestured to Annie, who was cowering inside the carriage. 'Get out. You can sit on the box — it's a fine day.' The girl tumbled out, and Collins reached down and threw her up to join the coachmen.

Samuel stared at Emma; then his eyes flicked towards the carriage and she scrambled back inside. He followed her and slammed the door. The coach rumbled forward and within a few yards began the difficult task of turning about so it could return to Town.

Even though the formidable man scowling at her from the other side of the interior was having difficulty containing his temper, Emma wasn't afraid of him, not in the way she'd been afraid of her father. However angry Samuel might be, he wouldn't raise his hand to her.

Once they were moving smoothly in the correct direction, she risked a glance at him from under her bonnet brim. His arms were folded across his chest, but he no longer looked so grim. To her astonishment his lips curved, and then he was laughing. This was the outside of enough. First he had manhandled her, and now he was finding her situation vastly entertaining.

'I see nothing funny about this, sir. My decision stands. Our engagement is at an end.'

His answer was to lean across and snatch her from the squabs. Ignoring her squeak of protest, he settled her on his lap. 'That's rubbish, and you know it, sweetheart. You love me as much as I love you, and there's nothing standing in our way apart from your ridiculous notions of propriety.'

She should struggle from his arms and insist that he place her back on the seat, but his warmth and solidity were melting her reserve. With a sigh she relaxed, and with his forefinger he tilted her face up to receive his kiss.

'Because of your escapade, we'll have to postpone our trip to Hertfordshire until after the party,' he said. 'By the time we return home today, the horses will be done in. I hope you're ashamed of yourself, young lady, for allowing your silly scruples to come between us.'

'I do love you; that has never been in doubt. However, we come from such different sections of society that our union is doomed to failure. We have nothing in common apart from an emotional attachment.'

'For an intelligent woman, you're being remarkably dense,' Sam remonstrated with her. 'It's not only ladies who improve their status by marriage. By marrying you, I immediately become elevated to the rank of gentleman, and will be accepted everywhere that you are. The fact that your family will ostracise us is a matter for celebration, not sadness.'

She wriggled off his lap and turned to face him. What he said made perfect sense, but she'd been so blinded by her fear that she'd failed to consider this eventuality. 'Are you now suggesting that I continue to refer to myself as Lady Emma?'

'I am indeed, my love. Once we're

wed, we'll return to Whitford Hall and I'll take over the running of the estate. Did you get around to sending the letter to Stokes informing him he was to remain in charge and move his family into the house?'

'I did not. There's been so much going on over the past few days that I had quite forgotten about it. And another thing — you never did buy me a riding horse.'

He chuckled, and with a casual flick undid the ribbon of her bonnet so it fell unheeded into the well of the carriage. 'I've had more pressing matters to deal with than finding you a mount. Anyway, as we'll be returning to Whitford Hall in a week or so, there's no need for the expense.'

She leant against him and he slid his arm around her waist. 'I'm sorry that I've put you to all this trouble, Samuel. I hardly slept at all last night, so by this morning I was overwrought and had begun to see things in a different light. I don't think we can return to Whitford

Hall scarcely six weeks after Richard died — even the most broad-minded of my neighbours would be scandalised at my indecent haste to marry again.'

'I'm tempted to say I don't give a damn about any of them, but understand we must live in harmony with our neighbours. Any children we might be blessed with need to be accepted, and for that reason alone I agree it would be wiser to remain away from Whitford for a few months.'

Emma yawned and her eyes began to droop. 'I should love to go abroad. Now the war is over, it must be safe to travel across the continent again.'

'In which case, that's what we shall do. Sleep now, darling. We've much to talk about when we get back.'

★   ★   ★

Sam, for the first time since he'd read Emma's letter of rejection, began to believe that he could still keep this wonderful woman in his life. His anger had been false; it had been sheer panic at the thought that he might be losing her that had made him so abrupt.

Losing her would have been far worse than the pain he'd felt when he'd been separated from his family. By some chance of fate, some miracle, she had come into his life and shown him how things might be. He'd never aspired to be a gentleman, never expected to be married because of his past, and now everything had changed.

He gazed down at this woman and swallowed a lump in his throat. Falling in love was another thing that was alien to him. Until now he'd believed it to be romantic nonsense, and not something a man would ever actually experience.

Gently he traced the shape of her lips with his finger, and she stirred a little beneath his touch. Immediately he removed his hand. She needed to sleep. He could do with a bit of shuteye himself, for all this galloping over the countryside had quite worn him out. His lips curved as he recalled how a couple of years ago he'd been marching all day carrying his backpack and been able to fight a battle at the end of it.

He was getting soft. Chasing villains in London just wasn't the same as fighting for king and country. He carefully lifted his feet and propped them against the opposite seat. His boots were mud-spattered, his breeches little better, and they would dirty the leather. Too bad — he had servants to take care of such matters nowadays.

If these were to be the last minutes of his life, he would die a contented man. He had never been happier than now, cradling the woman he loved in his arms and knowing that she felt the same way about him.

He'd sent a groom to his parents with a brief note explaining he would have to postpone his visit until the following week. Although disappointed, he'd waited ten years, so another few days wouldn't hurt him. It probably made more sense to get this Stanton business out of the way; then he could suggest that they remain in Sandridge until he and Emma were safely married.

He might not be as tough as he was when a serving soldier, but he was more than fit enough to take care of Emma and keep her safe from harm. He understood exactly why she'd fled. She was gently born and unused to complications of any kind.

'Samuel, I can't sleep until we've talked about why I ran away.' Emma wriggled upright but didn't move away from him. 'My thoughts were in such a tangle that I couldn't deal with it anymore. How are we to reconcile all the lies we've told? It is all such a dreadful muddle.'

'I've been thinking about it too,' he said. 'Do you like the house we're living in?'

'You know I do. Even though we had planned to run away to Norwich, now I think it better if we return to Whitford Hall eventually. However, the staff there met you as Sergeant Ross; they will find it difficult to accept you as Mr Rutherford, let alone as my husband.'

'It might be easier than you think, sweetheart. From what Collins told me, my parents are now well-to-do. Although this doesn't exactly make me a gentleman, I believe I would now be considered damn close to it. I think it would serve if we let it be known I've been using a false name because I'd been wrongly accused of a hanging offence.'

Emma clutched his hand and her eyes sparkled. 'I should have thought of this myself and saved us a deal of trouble. Far easier for everyone, including my unpleasant relations, to accept you as my husband if they think you were just pretending to be a member of the lower orders in order to avoid being arrested.'

'I suggest we explain the whole matter to Foster, and then he can tell the staff. The sale of your jewellery has given us more than enough blunt to remain in Town and live comfortably until we can return to Whitford Hall.

However, on reflection, I don't think there's enough to fund the trip abroad that you wanted.'

'I should be happy to remain in the country with your parents for as long as they are prepared to have us,' Emma said. 'I do not suppose your family has had the opportunity to see the sights in Town. The house in Tavistock Place is more than adequate to accommodate all of us.'

Her smile was radiant and sent a surge of heat to Sam's nether regions. He was obliged to hastily move her from his lap in order to hide his embarrassment. 'We must remain incognito until after the party tomorrow,' he said. 'Then we can make a prolonged stay in the country and reappear as Mr and Mrs Rutherford in a couple of months' time.'

'I rather think the ladies of the neighbourhood will relish the excitement when they are told. As long as they never discover we were not actually married, then I don't anticipate any difficulties.' She recovered her bonnet and, using the window glass as a mirror, carefully restored it to her curls. 'It feels as if I've spent several hours in this wretched vehicle, and am black and blue all over. I am relieved we will not be travelling any great distance until next week.'

Half an hour later, the coach turned under the archway and into the turning circle at the rear of the building. Sam opened the door and kicked down the steps. He jumped out, then reached in and swung Emma to the ground beside him. 'It's mid-afternoon already, and I'm sharp-set,' he said. 'I had no time to break my fast this morning. Can we dine early tonight, sweetheart?'

'I've not eaten anything either. I'll speak to Philips, but for now I am going upstairs to bathe and change. Shall we meet on the terrace at four thirty?'

'Dining *alfresco* again? That will be perfect for a summer's evening.' He watched her until she vanished into the house. God, how he loved that woman. Spending an evening alone with her was going to be purgatory — he just hoped he had sufficient self-control not to give in to his overwhelming desire to make love to her.

15

On Saturday Emma returned to her bedchamber in order to get ready for Benedict Stanton's party earlier than was strictly necessary. For some reason this event was scheduled to start at seven o'clock, which was odd as usually these kinds of soirées took place later in the evening in order to allow the guests time to dine before they came.

Samuel had decided not to tell the staff their story until tomorrow morning, so as far as Annie was concerned her mistress was just going to an ordinary social event. The fact that there were no footmen in the house could not have gone unnoticed, but as a household of this size really had no need for a footman at all, their absence would not add extra duties to the remaining staff.

'Are you quite sure you don't wish me to accompany you, Mrs Ashfield?'

Annie asked. 'I can take care of your reticule and spare slippers.'

'As far as I know there will be no dancing — this is a house-warming party not a ball. I expect there will be cards for the gentlemen and ladies who wish to play, and possibly some musical entertainment as well.'

Emma stepped into her evening gown and held her breath whilst her maid fastened the tiny buttons at the back. She had feared her increased appetite over the past three weeks might have made the bodice too small, but it still fit her well. The dress was made in the new style, the waistline under her bosom and the skirt flowing around her ankles. Annie handed her the loop that would hold the demi-train from beneath her feet whilst she was negotiating steps or dancing.

'That's ever so pretty, ma'am. Peach is the perfect colour for someone with your fair hair. I've never seen you look so grand. Mr Ashfield won't recognise you.'

This was hardly an appropriate comment, but Emma didn't take offence. Her maid meant well and had intended to pay a compliment. 'There is no need to wait up, Annie, as I have no idea what time we shall be returning. You may have the evening to yourself.'

The girl curtsied and handed over the matching fan and reticule; then with a smile she whisked away into the dressing room. Satisfied she looked her best, Emma made her way downstairs, glad that the evening was warm and she had no need to take a wrap or evening cloak.

She was halfway down the stairs when Samuel stepped from the shadows. She caught her breath. It was not she who was unrecognisable, but he. He was dressed in formal black, his hair cut short in the current fashion; and from his snowy-white neckcloth to his highly polished evening slippers, he was every inch a gentleman. He looked magnificent.

He bowed, and she all but ran down

the remaining stairs in order to throw herself into his arms. 'I cannot believe what a difference a haircut and new clothes have made to your appearance, my love,' she told him. 'I defy anybody at the party tonight to recognise you as Sergeant Ross.' She stepped back to admire him. 'Apart from the fact that you are more weather-beaten than most gentlemen, your appearance is fault-less.'

'If anyone remarks on that, I'll tell them the truth — that I served king and country for ten years. You can always tell a soldier by his complexion.'

Foster was waiting at the front door, which must mean the carriage was already outside. They were bowed out like royalty, and an unfamiliar coach-man handed Emma into the carriage. Once they were settled, she pointed towards the box and raised an eyebrow.

'An added precaution, sweetheart. He's from Bow Street.' Sam reached into his waistcoat pocket and handed her a small pistol. 'Put this in your bag.

It's primed and ready to fire. You'll not need it, but I'll be happier knowing you have it with you.'

Emma had no wish to take the nasty thing, but opened the drawstring on the neck of her reticule so he could drop it in. 'I dislike guns of any sort, but will take it if it makes you happier. There is nowhere you can hide a gun in that coat — do you have a weapon of your own?'

Sam opened his jacket and she saw he had a stiletto concealed in the lining. Her stomach lurched, and for the first time that evening she truly understood what they were about to do. This was no light-hearted social occasion, but a deadly serious — and possibly dangerous — attempt to find the proof necessary to bring the murderer of her husband to justice.

'Don't look so worried, sweetheart. I don't expect you to be involved in anything dangerous. Your role is to watch that Stanton is fully occupied, and if necessary engage him in conversation yourself. I can't see that he'd have any reason to go to his study, but I don't want to take any chances.'

'What are you hoping to find in there? Surely he would have destroyed any incriminating evidence by now.'

'One would have thought so, yes, but strangely enough that often isn't the case. When a villain thinks himself safe from retribution, and that he's too clever to be caught, he often keeps things that a more cautious person would burn.'

'I suppose he would have to keep the documentation relating to the stocks and shares that were transferred from Richard's business accounts,' Emma mused. 'My lawyers have a list at their Chelmsford office, and it would be easy enough to compare the two. Would that be enough to prove he was involved in something nefarious?'

'It would prove fraud, which is an offence that would get him transported. I doubt we'll ever find evidence related to the murder — only a complete nincompoop would hang on to the letter that was taken from your husband's study.'

'I wish we were actually on our way to a social engagement. Apart from my brief season, I've been to no events at all.'

Sam swore under his breath. 'Dammit to hell! You've led a miserable life up until now. Richard Stanton didn't physically abuse you; he kept you cloistered like a nun. I promise that things will be different once we're married — you may have as many callers as you want and go to as many parties as we have invitations to.'

'It's strange, my love, but until I met you a short time ago I had no idea that I was unhappy. My life at Whitford Hall was paradise compared to my life before I was married. Apart from the fact that I was never going to have children of my own, I thought myself reasonably content with my lot.'

'I'm going to make you happy, darling girl, and I vow that you'll never regret your decision to become my wife.'

The carriage rocked to a standstill behind a queue of other vehicles and they were obliged to wait until it was their turn to descend. 'Come,' said Sam, 'we'll put on a show and nobody will recognise us.'

'Samuel, I know neither of us have seen Mr and Mrs Forsyth, but do you think it possible one of them might have seen us?'

He linked her arm through his and patted her gloved hand. 'Not a chance, sweetheart. I doubt our own mothers would recognise us in our finery. Look, one of our men is taking the invitations at the door. That's a piece of luck and bodes well for tonight.'

He guided her up the front steps and handed in his invitation, restraining the impulse to wink at the young man who took it from him. He looked around with interest at the spacious entrance hall that led through an archway into an impressive reception room. Not quite big enough to be a ballroom, but a damn sight bigger than anything he'd ever been in as a guest before.

'We fit in perfectly, Samuel — elegant,

but not overdressed for the occasion. As there is no receiving line, I suppose we must wander about as we please. I think that fair-haired, self-satisfied-looking gentleman smirking over there is our host. He looks sufficiently like Richard to be his half-brother. I've no wish to speak to him, but I need to attach myself to another party if I'm not to be conspicuous when you slip away to investigate.'

'I can hear the sound of a piano being played,' Sam said. 'I'm sure you could find a seat in there without attracting unwanted attention.'

'If I do that, I'll not be able to keep an eye on Mr Stanton for you.'

'I don't think you need to. He looks settled for the evening and is enjoying the attention of his cronies. I'll be happier if I know you're safe; so indulge me, my love, and sit quietly and listen to the musical entertainment.'

Once Emma had settled on a daft gilt chair that would no doubt collapse under Sam if he tried to sit on one himself, he threaded his way back to the entrance hall, nodding and smiling at people as if he knew them. Unsurprisingly they responded, thus reinforcing his disguise.

As he'd hoped, the second footman from Tavistock Place was lurking with a tray of champagne in his hand. Sam walked over and, under the pretence of taking himself a glass, he asked his question. 'Is the study unoccupied, do you know?'

'I've not seen anyone go in, sir. You want to be careful, though — Forsyth is here, and he looks a nasty piece of work. He's wearing a purple and gold waistcoat, and is of middling height with light brown hair. You'll recognise him by the waistcoat.'

Sam picked up a glass and nodded his dismissal. The young man drifted away and was soon lost amongst the guests. Fortunately, his black evening clothes made him all but invisible in the shadows away from the light that flooded in from the long windows and open front door. When he was sure he was unobserved, he slipped down the corridor and flattened himself against the door of the study. There he listened carefully, heard nothing, and was as sure as he'd ever be that the room was empty. He reached behind him and turned the handle. The door opened silently behind him, and he was inside.

The room was much as he'd expected: book-lined walls, a bureau or two, and a large leather-topped desk to the left of the empty fireplace. This was the best place to start his search. He had his lock picks in case any of the drawers needed opening. He dropped to his knees, knowing that if anyone opened the door unexpectedly he would have time to duck out of sight.

* * *

After an excruciating few minutes, Emma decided she could stand it no longer and, like many others, stood and moved away from the appalling pianist. She drifted back into the main reception area and accepted a glass of lemonade when it was offered, then moved easily between the chattering groups, her ears attuned for any mention of Stanton or Forsyth. She found a convenient alcove behind a pillar and a pedestal with hothouse flowers, and moved into this temporary hiding place.

Stanton was still surrounded by admiring guests. Then she saw a nondescript sort of gentleman, apart from his hideous purple and gold waistcoat, urgently making his way towards the group. Something had disturbed this person, and she had a dreadful sinking feeling that it must have something to do with Samuel. She slipped through the crowd until she was lurking behind another pillar, hoping to hear what was said.

'Mr Stanton, I've just had word that there's a Bow Street Runner pretending to be an ostler in your stable yard. I don't like this at all. What do you want me to do?'

Emma held her breath and waited to hear Stanton's reply. 'You're letting your guilty conscience run away with you, Forsyth. I expect the man's supplementing his meagre income doing an extra day's work for me. But if you're concerned, make a tour of the house and check that there are no uninvited guests lurking about in corners.'

In her hurry to move away from Stanton's circle, Emma collided with a footman carrying a tray laden with glasses of champagne. The tray flew into the air and the glasses with it, and everyone in the vicinity was drenched, including Mr Forsyth, who had been about to go on his errand. Although her action had been unintentional, it had been the perfect distraction. Fortunately she had been untouched by the accident, and was able to slip away unnoticed during the squeals and complaints of the unfortunate ladies and gentlemen who had not been so lucky. She must warn Samuel that Forsyth was about to initiate a search of the house.

The noise and excitement had attracted attention and guests were moving rapidly towards the incident, allowing Emma to move in the opposite direction unnoticed. With luck, the footman from home would still be on duty collecting invitations from the latecomers and would be able to direct her to the study.

But unfortunately he was no longer in position, and the front doors were firmly closed. Emma looked around the space and decided to investigate a corridor in which there was a row of closed doors. She was about to open the first when someone spoke from right behind her.

'Can I help you, madam?'

Emma spun round and found herself face-to-face with the gentleman in the lurid waistcoat. 'I am looking for the ladies' retiring room. For some reason there are no maids on duty to direct me.' Somehow she managed to speak in her most disdainful manner, and immediately the man stepped away.

'The chamber you are seeking is up

the stairs. I beg your pardon for startling you.'

'Up the stairs, you say, sir? Those are hardly sufficient directions, and as you are obviously employed here I suggest that you escort me.' His startled expression at her raised voice would have made her smile if she weren't so frightened. Hopefully Samuel was nearby and would have heard them talking. She prayed this would be sufficient to keep him out of danger.

* * *

Sam used his lock pick to good effect, and was on his knees rummaging through the drawers of the desk when he heard Emma's voice outside. He froze. Whoever had accosted her had been persuaded to show her the retiring room. Hopefully this would give him sufficient time to complete his search.

He carefully closed the two drawers he'd searched, and the locks clicked back into place. Three more to open and look into, though he doubted he'd have time to investigate them all. He selected the middle drawer on the right-hand side and eased it open.

Fortune was smiling on them today, he thought, as he immediately picked up the letter from the lawyers informing Richard Stanton that someone was selling his stocks and shares. This was enough to make an arrest — there was no need to skulk about any more, for he had the evidence he needed.

He slipped the incriminating paper into his pocket and was about to close the drawer when he decided to risk delaying his exit in order to examine the other documents. Good God! These were the letters from the lawyer who'd acted as intermediary for Benedict Stanton in the theft of the stocks and shares. These joined the other papers in the cleverly concealed pocket he had had constructed in his new evening coat.

The drawer closed smoothly beneath his touch, and he was on his feet when he caught his breath. The door to the study was slowly opening. As an official investigator for the magistrate at Bow Street, he had every right to be there; but whoever was coming in would be desperate to save themselves from prosecution.

Flee or fight? He must somehow get out of the room and then make enough racket to bring guests and his two footmen running. He wished he'd got his pistol with him. Faced with a loaded gun, there were few men who would be brave enough to attack.

In one bound he placed himself behind the door so his presence would be concealed from whoever was coming in. The man stepped in and Sam shot forward, hitting him squarely in the small of his back with his shoulder. This gave him a vital few seconds to step over the prostrate form and escape into the corridor. He raced into the hall, determined to get out of the house with the evidence before he could be restrained.

He had the front door open when he remembered that tonight he wasn't alone. He hesitated. Should he go, and trust Emma's good sense to keep her safe — or remain, and risk capture and failing in his mission?

16

Emma was escorted as far as the bottom of the stairs. Then, unfortunately for her, a maid appeared, and the gentleman dashed off to continue his search. She prayed that Samuel would have had time to rejoin the guests in the few minutes she had been able to delay matters.

Having asked for the retiring room, she had no option but to visit it; but was in and out in moments and on her way downstairs when Samuel hurtled across the vestibule, flung open the front door, and then hesitated. Without any thought for her own safety, she raced down the stairs and was at his side when a roar of rage echoed across the hall.

'Quickly — we must make a run for it. I have what we need.' Samuel grabbed her arm, pulled her through the doorway, and slammed it behind him. 'We can't run from Cavendish Square to Tavistock Place. We'll have to duck round to the stable yard and find Collins and my other constable.'

Even with the demi-train of her dress held up by the band over her wrist, and the front of her skirt clutched in her other hand, Emma couldn't keep pace with him. Instead of slowing down, Sam snatched her up and threw her over his shoulder like a sack of coal. Although undignified, carrying her like this was efficient. They were under the arch and out of sight before the man pursuing them had reached the pavement. Sam had the good sense to put Emma down before they became an object of curiosity.

Collins, who must have been keeping watch, appeared immediately; and close behind him was an equally tough-looking individual. 'Trouble, Sergeant?'

'You could say that. I've got the papers I wanted; more than enough to send Stanton and his henchmen to the gallows. Is there somewhere secure Mrs Ashfield can remain whilst we arrest Forsyth and his employer?'

'If you go through the yard, madam, you'll see a narrow pathway — follow that and you'll come to an exit onto a busy thoroughfare. You'll be safe there.'

Emma wrenched open her reticule and removed the small pistol. 'Here, Samuel; you might find this useful. I certainly don't wish to have it in my possession any longer. I shall find myself somewhere to wait. Hopefully there will be an emporium of some sort I can browse in.'

He nodded, but his attention was no longer on her and she had no wish to distract him from what could be a dangerous task. She was halfway along the path when she realised this was a ridiculous suggestion. Most of the shops would be closing, if not already shut, and she was not in a promenade gown but her evening dress. She would look ridiculous.

So far she had managed to keep her

gown out of the dust, but her slippers were already ruined. She walked as briskly as she dared and emerged into the stable yard to find it deserted. Where on earth could she wait until Samuel returned for her?

She was about to investigate a closed door, hoping it might be a fodder or tack room, when she was suddenly seized in a cruel grip from behind.

'Well, well, what have we here? I reckon the master will be right pleased with me for catching you.' The man twisted her arm so violently that an excruciating pain made her cry out. 'There'll be more of the same if you struggle or make a sound.'

★   ★   ★

Sam and his two assistants made their way to the arch, and he gestured for them to remain concealed behind the brickwork. 'Forsyth will have realised I'm not alone. He'll have found others to help him.' As he waited, listening, he noted a loose brick in the wall above him. He pulled out the documents and jammed them into the space behind the brick and then replaced it. Better to have these vital documents safe and secure just in case things didn't go his way.

His men had cudgels, while he had only his knife and the little gun meant to be used by a lady. He closed his eyes for a second and steadied his breathing as he had always done before a battle. His nerves settled, he focused on the sound of cautious footsteps approaching their hiding place. He glanced across and Collins nodded — he'd heard them coming too. Then there was no time for further thought as Forsyth and two other rough individuals burst through the archway. Samuel's fist connected with the leader's jaw, and the man folded like a marionette with broken strings. The other two were dealt with in similar fashion. The entire process had taken less than a minute and, thank God, attracted no unwanted attention from any other ne'er-do-wells who might be working in the stables.

'We'll truss them up and toss them in the tack room,' Sam said. 'Bolt the door and secure it with whatever you can find.' He addressed the constable directly. 'Smith, when we're done, borrow a horse and get to Bow Street — we need reinforcements and a cart to remove the prisoners.'

The man touched his cap. 'Righto, Sergeant.'

It took the three of them longer than it should have to gag, tie and incarcerate the three they'd captured. Smith selected a handsome bay mare and moments later clattered out of the yard. As Sam brushed the dirt from his once-immaculate evening rig, he heard a clock in a local church strike eight. As the last note died away, he swore.

'Dammit to hell! We sent my wife on a fool's errand. The shops will be closed and she will be horribly conspicuous in her evening gown. What was I thinking of?'

Collins's colour faded to a pasty white. 'Buggeration! I'll get down there now and bring her back.'

'There's no need to do that,' came a low voice from the doorway. 'I have her safe inside.'

Sam turned to find himself facing two men, one scruffy, the other he recognised as Benedict Stanton. Somehow they'd captured Emma. If they harmed a hair on her head, they would live to regret it. Sam thought that if he could delay matters for an hour or so, then reinforcements would arrive and this situation could be turned to his advantage.

Although he had the papers safely hidden, now that Stanton had involved himself personally in the matter, his days of freedom were numbered. Kidnapping was a capital offence. The man was obviously deranged; hadn't thought this through. Unless he was prepared to murder all three of them, he couldn't escape justice.

Sam moved smoothly away from the

tack room door, praying that Stanton wouldn't realise his other three henchmen were tied up inside. Sam was fairly sure they would remain unconscious for a while longer, so even if they were released they wouldn't be much use to their employer.

'Stanton, I presume. I'm Sergeant Ross of Bow Street, and you're under arrest for theft, murder and kidnapping.' He maintained eye contact as he spoke, knowing that he looked a formidable and dangerous opponent. Would it be enough to bluff his way out of this?

Stanton's triumphant sneer slipped and the gun in his hand wavered. Sam launched himself, and his head connected with the man's throat, sending him reeling backwards. The gun went off harmlessly, but the noise of the retort almost deafened him.

After that it was easy. Stanton and the other individual were hogtied and dumped in with their companions in crime. 'Collins, reload the pistol if you can find powder and shot, and stand guard,' Sam instructed.

'Won't you want to take it, Sergeant?'

'No, I've got this. It wouldn't hit a barn door from further than a yard, but it's better than nothing.' He showed him the small gun and then straightened his jacket, checked that his cravat was relatively unscathed by his fisticuffs, and entered the house at a run. He needed to collect the two footmen before he searched for Emma. It was unlikely there was more than one person guarding her, but he wasn't going to take any chances.

Inside, the party was continuing, and laughter and loud voices filled the passageways. Sam forced himself to stroll and not march. He must remain in his assumed persona as a gentleman in order not to attract unwanted attention.

He paused for a moment to get his bearings, imagining the layout of the building which he'd learnt from the blueprints. Emma wouldn't be put anywhere near the main reception areas just in case a guest blundered into the chamber in which she was held. He would try the study first and then widen his search. Sam didn't want to go back into the crush of guests in order to look for his footmen, but he would dearly like to have them at his back. Not wanting to delay any longer, he moved silently to the study and pressed his ear against the door.

* * *

Emma was forced through a side door and along a passageway, then bundled into the study. Her captor shoved her across the room and into an armchair.

'You sit here, missy, and don't make a sound if you know what's good for you. Bloody stupid, if you ask me, bringing along a flash moll like you. I would have thought a runner'd have more sense.'

These remarks didn't require a reply, so Emma did as she was told and sat quietly. The man cuffed her hard around the face, making her dizzy; and she was almost sure she heard him talking to somebody outside the door. By the time she'd recovered, he was back by her side looking menacing.

She cowered into the chair, hoping her obvious submission might dissuade him from striking her again. The more he hurt her, the greater chance there was that Samuel would do something violent to avenge her. No doubt in his official capacity, he had a certain leeway when it came to apprehending miscreants, though she'd no wish for her future husband to have more blood on his hands than was strictly necessary.

The inside of her mouth was salty; cautiously she ran her tongue around her lips and tasted blood. Dare she reach into her reticule and remove her handkerchief, or would this action promote further blows?

Before she could decide, the study door opened and Benedict Stanton stepped in. He strode over to her, and this time her fear was genuine. He might be a macaroni, but his eyes were hard, and she knew him to be more dangerous than he appeared. He wouldn't hesitate to murder her if he discovered her true identity.

'Who are you, madam, and what are you doing at my party?'

'I am Mrs Ashfield. My husband's a Bow Street investigator, and I accompanied him tonight, as he could not gain entry on his own.' Her voice was commendably even, her fear not apparent from her speech.

Stanton's face changed and his eyes glittered with something terrifying. He kicked the chair, almost tipping it over. 'How many men has he got with him?'

Emma shook her head. 'We came, like everyone else, to attend your party. My husband just wanted to mingle in order to gain information. He wouldn't have brought me along otherwise.'

This sounded plausible, and she hoped he'd believe her. The sound of her heart hammering in her ears made concentrating almost impossible. This was the man who'd stolen all of Richard's money; the man whose employee had murdered her husband.

Stanton looked half-convinced, but then he scowled and rushed to the desk. He removed a small key from his pocket and opened a desk drawer. The rustling of paper filled the room and Emma held her breath. He was going to discover that Samuel had taken the documents, and then . . . and then heaven knew what would happen to her.

She expected him to slam the drawer; to curse and storm across to her. But what he did was far more frightening. Slowly he straightened, and then his mouth curved in a facsimile of a smile. 'I believe your husband has something that belongs to me. I'm certain he will be willing to exchange it for your life.' He turned to his minion. 'Remain here with her. I'm going to fetch her husband.'

Stanton had abandoned his foppish persona and Emma saw him as he truly was — an evil and insane monster. The minutes dragged as she waited for him to return. She prayed Sam would not be captured too. Hardly daring to breathe, she kept her eyes fixed to the door as she tried desperately to think of a way she could prevent Stanton from killing them both in order to regain the missing papers. She wasn't tied to her chair: her hands and feet were free; and she was perfectly able to scream if she thought that might help.

The noxious odour coming from the man who had captured her was no longer as obvious. She thought this meant he was not standing directly behind her. Was this her opportunity to escape? She tensed her limbs and gripped the arms of the chair, intending to use them to propel herself forwards and pray that she reached the door before the villain reacted.

As she shot out of the chair, the door flew open and Samuel appeared. 'Get down, sweetheart — now!' he shouted.

Emma dropped to her knees and a shot whistled over her head. She crouched on the floor, making herself as small as possible, and hoping that Samuel's aim was true.

The heavy thud of a body falling to the floor told her it was safe to rise, but for some reason her legs would not respond to her command.

'It's over, sweetheart. Here, let me help you up.' She was lifted to her feet and Sam's arms enfolded her. 'Don't look round; I'll take you somewhere you can rest until our carriage arrives. Nothing more needs doing here.'

She leaned against him, unable to respond with more than a nod. He gently guided her from the room, and once she was in the passageway her voice returned.

'I don't want to stay another minute in this house, Samuel. I shall wait outside for the carriage.'

He didn't argue. A familiar face was there to open the door. 'Lock the study door,' Sam said, 'and tell the butler the party's over. Mr Stanton has been arrested.'

The footman grinned. 'Them folk in there won't notice, Mr Ashfield. They only came to have a good time.'

'If the guests are evicted,' Emma said, 'there will be chaos in the square, as none of them will have any transport home. Why not let things continue?' This was the first time she'd looked directly at the footman, and his happy smile vanished and his eyes widened. She had forgotten her injuries — they must be worse than she'd realised. Maybe it would be better to remain inside until the carriage came.

'Is there a chamber we can use where we won't be disturbed?' Emma asked the footman.

'I'll take you to an anteroom, Mrs Ashfield. It's just across the hallway.'

The young man showed them into a prettily decorated chamber; one that must have been used by the lady of the house to entertain her morning callers. 'I'll sit by the window, Samuel; then I can see when it's time to leave.'

Once Emma was seated, Sam kissed

the top of her head and then spoke in a low voice to the footman before returning to crouch anxiously at her side. 'I've sent for warm water and clean cloths. I'll do my best to clean you up. I don't think you'll require sutures.'

'What I would really like, my love, is some refreshment. Although my mouth is sore, it's not painful enough to prevent me from eating.'

His eyes blazed and his hands tightened on hers. 'I'll never forgive myself. I shouldn't have allowed you to accompany me. All this could have been achieved with a search warrant; there was no need for the play-acting and — '

'Hush, my dear. I don't regret a moment of it. If I hadn't insisted on coming to London, we would not be getting married in a week or two. Even if we'd failed — if Stanton had taken everything, we would still have emerged the victors, as we now have each other.'

Sam regained his feet, carried over a straight-backed chair, and placed it beside hers. 'I've sent for a cart and constables; they should be here in an hour. The papers we needed to prove Stanton had stolen your money are hidden in the stable yard. I'll recover them before we leave.'

There was a soft tap on the door and the footman came in with a tray of items Sam had thought necessary to tend to Emma's injuries. 'Put the tray on that side table. We'd like coffee and something to eat. Presumably there's a buffet supper being served later — bring us a selection from that.'

After a painful few minutes, Sam had cleaned Emma's face and was satisfied she wouldn't need the attention of a physician. 'I'm afraid you're going to have a black eye, sweetheart, but the swelling around the cut on your lip should be gone by tomorrow. You're going to have to stay indoors until you look respectable. Looking as you do, our neighbours will think I attacked you.'

'I can wear that hideous bonnet with a brim like a coal scuttle — I defy anyone to see my face if I have that on my head.' Emma laughed. 'And anyway, I shall be perfectly content to remain indoors with you.'

His smile made her toes curl, and only the arrival of the second tray prevented him from kissing her. The food was delicious, and she managed to mumble her way through a prodigious amount of it. The carriage pulled up outside before the constables and cart had come to remove the prisoners.

'I am perfectly able to return home on my own, Samuel,' said Emma. 'You must remain here and do your duty.'

'This is the last task I'll perform for Bow Street. Once this matter has been dealt with by the magistrate, I shall hand in my resignation.'

'I cannot wait to begin our new life together, my dear. Although you know little about running an estate, I am sure after a few months you will have everything in hand. Once we are in residence, our tenants will be all the better for having you in charge.'

He escorted her to the carriage and

lifted her in. On the journey home, she had ample opportunity to consider how tonight's escapade had changed everything. Benedict Stanton was no longer a problem, and what he had stolen would be returned. She hoped it wouldn't take more than a week or two, as once she was married and no longer a Stanton, it was possible there might be difficulties regaining control of the missing funds.

Emma was quite certain that Samuel was aware of this too. He might insist they delay their nuptials until the lawyers had completed their investigations and the money had been restored. However, this was not an option Emma was prepared to contemplate. The longer it took for them to be married, the more time there was for Samuel to reconsider his position. He loved her as much as she loved him; but if he for a moment believed she would be better off without him, then he would vanish from her life as quickly as he'd come into it. She had no option but to take matters into her own hands.

Sam recovered the hidden documents and supervised the transfer of the prisoners. He intended to borrow a nag from the stables so he could accompany the constables and cart to Bow Street. The corpse was dumped in with the living and would be disposed of by the constables.

Collins pointed out a serious flaw in this plan. 'You can't ride in that getup, Sergeant. You ain't got no boots on.'

'I'll have to wait for our carriage to return for me, and then I'll change and join you at Bow Street.'

'No need to do that, sir. If you give me them papers, I'll tell the Beak what's what and get the prisoners logged in. You get on home, Sergeant. You'll not be needed until the morning.'

Unless he was prepared to travel in the cart with the prisoners, Sam knew he had no option but to agree with Collins. He returned to the house and paced the floor of the anteroom until his transport eventually returned. The light was fading by the time he arrived at Tavistock Place, and he heard a clock strike ten.

Foster was waiting to let him in and informed him that Emma had retired. Sam decided he might as well go up himself, as he had no wish to remain in his ridiculous clothes a moment longer than he had to. Benton had been given the evening off, so he would have his apartment to himself.

He pushed open the door to his sitting room and was surprised to find light flickering from his bedchamber. He strode across and stepped in, his heart slamming in his chest. Emma was stretched out on his bed, still wearing her evening gown.

'At last! I thought you were never going to return.' Gracefully she swung her bare feet to the floor and stood up. 'This gown is impossible to remove without assistance, and I gave Annie the evening off.'

She turned, and Sam had no option

but to approach. He viewed with alarm the tiny silk-covered buttons that ran from the top to the bottom of Emma's close-fitting bodice. Fiddling with those damn things was going to take all his self-control, and he wasn't sure he'd be able to prevent himself from making love to her.

When he had the last button undone, his hands were shaking; he thought she would thank him and leave. Instead, she slowly turned and allowed the gown to slither from her shoulders, leaving her standing in front of him in nothing but her petticoats.

Her eyes told him all he needed to know, and he closed the gap between them. 'Are you quite sure, my darling? For once I start to make love to you, I'll not be able to stop.'

'As we are to be married in a week or so, my love, I hardly think it matters. I love you, and I've no wish to wait a moment longer to show you just how much.'

We do hope that you have enjoyed reading this large print book.

Did you know that all of our titles are available for purchase?

We publish a wide range of high quality large print books including:
**Romances, Mysteries, Classics
General Fiction
Non Fiction and Westerns**

Special interest titles available in large print are:
**The Little Oxford Dictionary
Music Book, Song Book
Hymn Book, Service Book**

Also available from us courtesy of Oxford University Press:
**Young Readers' Dictionary
(large print edition)
Young Readers' Thesaurus
(large print edition)**

For further information or a free brochure, please contact us at:
**Ulverscroft Large Print Books Ltd.,
The Green, Bradgate Road, Anstey,
Leicester, LE7 7FU, England.
Tel:** (00 44) **0116 236 4325
Fax:** (00 44) **0116 234 0205**

Other titles in the
Linford Romance Library:

INTRIGUE IN ROME

Phyllis Mallett

Gail Bennett's working holiday in Rome takes an unexpectedly sinister turn as soon as she arrives at her hotel. Why does the receptionist give out her personal details to someone on the phone? Who is the mysterious man she spies checking her car over? Soon she meets Paul, a handsome Englishman keen to romance her — but he is not what he seems. And how does Donato — Italian, charming — fit into the picture? Gail knows that one of them can save her, while the other could be the death of her . . .

THE FAMILY AT CLOCKMAKERS COTTAGE

June Davies

Feeling bereft after her sister Fanny gets married and moves away, young Amy Macfarlene must manage Clockmakers Cottage on her own, while earning a living as a parlour maid and seamstress for a wealthy local family, the Paslews. Her wayward brother Rory is a constant concern, as he is clearly embroiled in some shady dealings and refuses all offers of help. Amy's childhood sweetheart Dan is a comfort to her — but as her friendship with the handsome Gilbert Paslew grows, so do her uncertainties about her future . . .

RACHEL'S FLOWERS

Christina Green

Rachel Swann takes a sabbatical from her London floristry job to come home and temporarily manage the family plant nursery. But then it emerges that her uncle has also asked the globetrotting plant collector Benjamin Hunter to do the self-same task! Wary of Ben's exotic plans for the establishment, Rachel is determined to keep the nursery running in its traditional manner. But as the two work together, they cannot ignore the seeds of a special relationship slowly blooming between them . . .